I0687353

# Vegan Zombie Apocalypse

## By Wol-vriey

# Vegan Zombie Apocalypse

By Wol-vriey

**Burning Bulb**
PUBLISHING

**Vegan Zombie Apocalypse**
by **Wol-vriey**

Burning Bulb Publishing
P.O. Box 4721
Bridgeport, WV 26330-4721
United States of America
*www.BurningBulbPublishing.com*

Cover designed by Gary Lee Vincent with the following licensed elements from Fotolia:
- suffering woman © konradbak
- old potato with sprouting shoots © dimedrol68

First printing.

Paperback Edition ISBN: 978-0-61577-282-0

Printed in the United States of America

Library of Congress Control Number: 2013936095

# Foreword

By Rich Bottles Jr.

Author of "Lumberjacked,"
"Hellhole West Virginia,"
and "The Manacled"

---

Burning Bulb Publishing doesn't openly solicit novel submissions, since the company was primarily set up as a cooperative between a small group of West Virginia authors who assist each other in producing the co-op's rather eclectic line of titles, but Burning Bulb does sometimes delve into the current popular niche of publishing transgressive short story anthologies. This is how we first encountered Wol-vriey.

According to his author biography on Amazon, "Wol-vriey is Nigerian and quite tall. You may know him from such emails as: 'Your MILLIONAIRE Uncle just passed away and needs to wire your inheritance in the next three days! Please provide your bank's routing number and account number to...'

"When he's not handling the legalities of your Uncle's estate, he likes to style his threatening-to-thin-beyond-redemption hair and chase things that go bump in the night. Wol-vriey recycles the ridiculous into reasonable reality for the reader."

Wol-vriey's work was recently featured in the Burning Bulb Publishing anthologies "The Big

Book of Bizarro" and "Westward Hoes." His ability to capture the true essence and spirit of the bizarro fiction genre is obvious in these anthologies and his short stories quickly become fan favorites. Consequently, when Wol-vriey asked Burning Bulb to consider publishing a zombie novel he had finished, the offer was hard to resist.

I am not unfamiliar with the zombie horror genre, although my own work has only utilized zombies as peripheral plot elements. But I often find myself boasting to fellow horror fans that I'm proud to have kin buried at the Evans City, Pennsylvania, cemetery where the original "Night of the Living Dead" was filmed back in 1968. Even though I was only six years old when the movie debuted, I grew up attending sporadic screenings of the movie at local drive-ins and staying up late on Saturday nights to watch annual broadcasts of the film on Chilly Billy's (a.k.a. "Bill Cardille's") Chiller Theater on WIIC-TV.

Consequently, I was a bit skeptical when Wol-vriey announced that his latest bizarro novel had a zombie theme. I wondered if it was even possible to create something new and original in a genre that has basically been rehashing a public domain film for the past 45 years. But if anyone can do it, certainly Wol-vriey is capable, and he did not disappoint me.

When I read that Wol-vriey's zombies of the future were evolving to the point of becoming vegetarians, I realized I was experiencing something truly unique in the zombie genre. Of course, the zombies still pose a formidable threat to mankind, since the zombies use the fertile bodies of their human captives to cultivate their blood-infused veggies. Without giving too much away, Wol-vriey manages to give a whole new meaning to the phrase "brain *eating* zombies."

A thoughtful reader could easily make the observation that the underlying theme of Vegan Zombie Apocalypse is an indictment of religious intolerance and hypocrisy, but I doubt Wol-vriey even wants anyone to look at this novel too deeply, since the book's obvious goal is simply to entertain.

In addition to holding down a day job, I review quite a few manuscripts for Burning Bulb Publishing, and it can be a chore at times, but the difficulty I experienced while working with "Vegan Zombie Apocalypse" was that I found myself wanting to read the book purely for entertainment rather than professionally editing it for publication. That is why I also asked local Fairmont, WV, proof-reader Teresa Pollack to take a look at the book after I finished my initial edit.

In conclusion, "Vegan Zombie Apocalypse" is one of the best bizarro novels I have ever read, but its appeal should extend far beyond the burgeoning bizarro fan base. Enthusiasts of Science Fiction, Fantasy and Horror, and especially zombie fiction lovers, should relish this book, even though it ventures into the dark realm of the extraordinarily grotesque at times, many times actually.

So, grab yourself a bag of blood-potato chips and a cold glass of Dr. October, take a seat on your favorite meat chair, and enjoy this fucked up joy ride of an adventure.

# Prologues

## 1. *Able Kane and Morphia*

"The world is perfectly okay as it is," Morphia told Able Kane. "It doesn't *need* to be better."

Able shook his head. "I disagree. Even perfection can often be improved upon. Our way of life is far from perfect."

Morphia smiled her corpse's smile back at him. "Imperfection is the new perfection, darling. Live with it."

"I can't accept reality as blithely as you do... I find your unquestioning..."

Morphia sighed. Able was the living definition of boring at times. To shut him up, she freed his cock from his pants and stuffed it into her mouth.

## 2. Soil

Soil dreamt of the boltgun every night. This wasn't unusual--every humancow dreamt this dream--the nightmare of their 'last walk' to the slaughterhouse at the far end of the farm. The older one got, the more frequent it became.

The walk to the *rest in pieces.*

Soil's dream never varied. In it, she was chewing her mother's roast liver (occasionally it was her kidney), and laden with ripe blood-potatoes, wearily making her way down the path, her soles crunching smooth pebbles. She was so tired of her burdensome body; all she wanted was rest... rest... rest.

In the slaughterhouse, the foreman first checked to ensure she was properly ripe. Then she took her place on the conveyor, lying on her back with her head touching the dirty cracked soles of the mancow or womancow ahead of her. After her, the girl behind her lay on the conveyor, her head against Soil's feet.

The conveyor moved at an even pace, clanking slightly as it rolled over its gears. It was a jerky ride; every few feet it stopped and shuddered as a humancow ahead of her died.

With each transmitted death, pleasant anticipation built in Soil. It wouldn't be long now till she'd rest for good.

Then the humancow ahead of her kicked her in the head in her death throes, and she realized she was next.

She was calm. She would not make a nuisance of herself. She intended being a shining example of livestock death.

She smiled as the boltgun was swung against her head, smiled at the dead-eyed vegan slaughterer as he set the muzzle above her ear and pulled the trigger.

Soil never felt her own death--she was well outside of herself by then. She shat and peed herself as humancows usually did when dying.

Then the scoop guillotine descended and removed her brain.

# Part One:
# The Womancow

# Chapter 1

Soil-15f was twenty-five years old. She was five feet six inches tall, and pretty.

Had her body been visible beneath the lush foliage obliterating it from view, she would have been brown-skinned and considered a shapely woman.

As it was now, she looked like a tree that had decided to walk around.

With the exclusion of her face, palms, and the soles of her feet, Soil was covered from head to toe by potato creepers. Their leaves formed a dense additional layer of covering over the first.

Soil was a womancow, a female humancow. She was part of the herd of Vegfarm 642, one of the largest vegfarms supplying blood potatoes to Neo La.

She'd been on the farm two years.

Humancows were meatsoil creatures, bred solely for the cultivation of the zombie staple, blood potatoes.

Once the potatoes planted in Soil's flesh ripened, she would be scheduled for harvesting.

In her case, three years from now.

No humancow survived harvesting; the potato tubers were too deeply inserted into the flesh of the meatfield they were grown in.

Because the zombies--the vegans--were humane, all humancows were killed first, then the tubers were dug out of them.

Soil didn't want to die, but knew death was inevitable. From the moment of capture and conversion to livestock, all humancows knew death was the only freedom they would ever have from potato pain.

And her tubers hurt--each pained her like a headache. Some tubers had grown their roots into her nerve tracts and hurt like toothaches.

The painkillers the zombies provided daily took the edge off the pain, but only just.

#

Soil walked over to the cafeteria, an un-walled chamber fifty meters per side. Spitted corpses roasted over blazing fires in cooking pits situated below regularly spaced holes in the ceiling.

The fires were tended by zombie servers. Soil walked past a pit where four zombies in protective rubber clothing were removing the spit from the ass of a delicious smelling corpse.

Inside their protective clothes the zombies were tall and bald, with decaying skin and blank eyes.

The corpse they worked on was full of holes--large tunnels through its muscles where its potatoes had been removed. It looked like it had been burrowed through by rodents.

Soil thought it odd how you only saw naked bodies when they were being cooked.

She stopped a moment and watched the zombie cooks work. They jerked the spit out and set the sizzling corpse on a metal tray. A zombie with a meat cleaver began cutting it into smaller chunks.

Soil watched them force a metal spike between the buttocks of another humancow corpse. She stared entranced while the zombies worked the spike up into the torso. What fascinated her was the way the potato holes let her monitor the spit's jerky progress up through the body.

Finally the tip of the skewer exited the corpse's neck and the zombies raised it up above the fire to roast.

Soil licked her lips and walked over to her favorite table.

Two others were seated there--Soil-219f and Earth-15m, both Soil's friends. Other than facial recognition, you could tell who was who by the ID numbers tattooed in black on their foreheads.

219f was fat. The vegans liked fat humancows because they provided a greater body surface to grow tubers in. 15m was male and slim like Soil.

Soil liked it that she and 15m were friends, seeing as their numbers matched.

They'd also been brought to the farm and implanted on the same day two years before. Like Soil, 15m had three more years to go before his potato crop would ripen for harvesting.

(There were two thousand humancows on Vegfarm 642--a thousand each of male and female. Their numbers went from 1f to 999f for females and 1m to 999m for males.

Their numbers were recycled--once a humancow was killed and processed, her or his replacement received their number.

All females were named Soil; all males, Earth. All thought of themselves as 'Soil' or 'Earth' and others as numbers.

The postscript letters were important because humancows lacked facial hair and with their covering of vines, it was occasionally impossible to tell male from female by sight alone.)

#

Most humancows in the cafeteria were seated talking to one another. Those scheduled to die within a few days walked aimlessly about between tables, their minds addled by the increased amount of medications the zombies had fed them to prevent the increased amount of potato poisons in their systems from addling their minds.

Watching them, Soil shuddered. One day she'd be in their shoes. That day being years distant didn't alter the fact of its horror.

Soil sat with her friends. 15 passed her a plate of meat. She looked it over and chose a roast hand. She pulled off the cracked fingernails, then bit through the crisp skin into the delicately spiced flesh.

"This is good food," she said to make conversation.

"Food's always good here," 15 said. "The vegans take good care of us."

"The vegans only keep us healthy because if we're ill their potatoes will suffer," 219 said.

"Sshhhh," 15 said. He looked around to ensure no one had overheard their conversation. "Talk like that gets you processed early."

"He's right," Soil said, biting deeply into the palm-meat of the hand she was eating. "You'll be branded a troublemaker and killed early."

"I don't want to die," 219 retorted. "I don't want to end up as food for--"

"Everyone's food," Soil retorted in turn. She waved the hand she was eating at them. "Whoever this was most likely died last week, maybe even yesterday. It's the way of the world. Eat and be eaten."

"Yeah," 15 said. "We'll all be fucking eaten sooner or later. It's not just us either. Remember the necros eat the vegans."

"That's just a rumor," Soil said. She picked the hand clean of flesh, then selected a quarter of a heart from the meat tray. She bit into this, enjoying the spurt of juice over her rotting teeth--the zombies weren't too hot on Medicare. "The vegans are too tough for the damned necros; else the cunts would have rescued us long ago so they can kill us themselves."

219 nodded. She never liked this line of reasoning, but it had to be true. Why else was it that no one ever bothered to come help them?

She pointed to the twenty-foot-high walls enclosing them, with the zombie sentry patrols walking along the barbed wire fences.

"There has to be something better than this shitty existence we're in."

"There isn't," 15 said brutally. "Fucking get used to it and stop whining."

He dropped his voice to a whisper as two zombies rolled a trolley over to their table and started heaping sizzling meat onto their trays. 15 fished a dripping forearm out of the tray and took a bite.

"Look, we all lived out in the worlderness before. That was hell, what with those necros shithead fanatics killing everyone. So we were free, but there also wasn't any food."

"Now we're captives and have food to spare." Soil finished for him.

"More like *we are* food," 219 said loudly. "Fuck this asshole life. I want out of here yesterday! I want my freedom back!"

Soil and 15 stiffened. The zombies had to have heard that. All the humancows at the surrounding tables stopped eating in shock.

The zombie servers looked at each other and laughed as at a private joke. They lifted a huge thigh from the trolley and dropped it in front of 219. It fell with a thud, splattering juice all over her leaves.

One of the zombies bent down close to her, its horrible dead eyes portable nightmares. "Eat up, womancow," it said. "You should be grateful we vegans are so concerned about human welfare."

219 now realized her outburst had been overheard. She realized the implications. All the humancows at the surrounding table made a show of eating their food.

Soil and 15 didn't, but didn't say anything.

"I didn't mean it like that," 219 said, running both hands worriedly through her scalp leaves.

"Of course you didn't, fat womancow," the zombie said nicely. "Of course you didn't."

He noted her ID number and they rolled their trolley to another table to serve roast meat.

#

"That stupid heifer," 15m told Soil when they were alone, seated on a bench outside the cafeteria. Their leaf covering made them look like tree branches that had fallen on the benches. "How could she? She's still got two years to go before the slaughterhouse."

Soil glanced across the farmyard at the slaughterhouse. "Not any more, she hasn't," she said. "I saw the way the zombies looked at each other when they left us. We'll be eating her by next week."

"Serves the dumb cow right."

Soil looked at 15, her eyes teary. "I don't know how it is with you, but I can't go on living like this, just marking time till time's up. 219 was right--I'm not cut out to be food. We've got to do something."

15 smiled grimly. "*We are* going to do something." He looked around quickly to ensure no one was either near them or gazing in their direction. Then he pulled something from his hip foliage, and quickly handed it to Soil.

She peered at it and gasped. "A multikey? Where'd you get this?"

"Just hide it in your cuntbag," he said. "It's our key out of this hell."

Eyes still wide with shock, Soil nodded. She stuck her hands into the leaf growth obscuring her groin, and pushed her vines aside until she felt her vaginal zip. She undid this, pushed the key into her sex and zipped it up again.

"It's safe now," 15 said with relief. "I've been hiding it in a hollowed waist tendril. I can't keep it up my ass because it's certain to drop out when I shit."

"How'd you get it?"

"I stole it. I was deputized to help sterilize yesterday, when the conveyors broke down in the power plant. Two zombies accidentally ripped their suits while handling brains and the vegan remains jammed the gears. You know how once there's any threat of brain contamination, the zombies use us to clear shit up? At one point I was locked in with the corpses. I quickly rifled through their pockets and found the key. There were actually two, but taking both would have looked very suspicious."

"What now?"

15's face was grim. "Once I can get hold of some brains and a hoverbike, I'm leaving this shithole. You coming?"

She nodded. "Where'll we go?"

"Everywhere but here."

# Chapter 2

Vaginas are storage compartments.

After taking her medicine the next morning, Soil unzipped her cunt and took out the multikey. She studied it for a while. It would open any door on the farm, possibly any door anywhere in Neo La, the capital of the vegan DEZA Empire.

Staring at the key, unusual hope flooded Soil. It *was* possible. She could escape and not wind up as food.

She looked around the dorm, saw two womancows come in and sit on their straw beds. She replaced the multikey between her legs and zipped herself up again.

Vaginas are storage compartments.

None of the humans on Vegfarm 642 ever had sex. EVER. It wasn't that it was forbidden or that their sex organs were either missing or didn't work.

No, it was that the drugs the vegans provided to dull potato pain were even more effective at killing libido than their intended purpose.

Soil had no idea if this was intentional. What she did know was that with no sex about to happen anywhere, new uses had been found for women's cunts.

So every womancow on Vegfarm 642 had a (zombie-provided) cuntbag, the modern female personal accessory which had replaced the ancient ladies' handbag. With no children to bear, the redundant womb was included in the conversion package.

In their cuntbags, womancows kept their secrets.

# 

The vultures swooped, but not on the anticipated carcass.

Soil was startled when 219 ran into the dorm.

"The undead have taken 15m away" she gasped, upon reaching Soil.

Pure undiluted fear filled Soil.

"*Taken?* What did they say he did?"

219 took a long moment to get her breath back before replying.

When she did reply, however, the look on her face was awestruck.

"The rumor is that someone on their work detail stole a multikey."

She smiled dreamily. "Shee-it! That I could be so fucking lucky--my ass would be out of here like a bolt of lightning".

Reality crash-landed her to the farm again. "The zombies have gotten it wrong anyway--whoever stole their damn key, it clearly wasn't 15--everyone on the farm knows what a damn conformist he is."

Soil heaved a heavy sigh of relief, which 219 interpreted to be one of shared disgust at 15's spinelessness.

She'd been terrified when 219 began talking. But once reminded of how everyone viewed her male numbersake, she realized there was no chance of their being found out.

The zombies would never believe 15 capable of stealing their key. They were still getting the fuck out of this shithole the first chance they fucking got.

She ran her hands through the green tangle of creepers forming her hair, then smiled at 219. "Let's hit the cafeteria--I'm ravenous. I could totally binge on some girl-tripe now.

#

Feasting on roast girl intestines in the cafeteria, Soil and 219 kept their ears peeled for any info they could glean about the arrests.

Another girl, 69, so decorated with creepers Soil couldn't imagine her living any longer than two weeks at the outside, came and sat beside them, bearing a plate of roast penises.

Before ending up at Vegfarm 642, 69 had been gang-raped and left for dead--it was *because* she'd been out cold that the zombies had caught her.

For 69, eating roast cocks was her way of getting payback. It was the only food she ever ate.

*It's a fucked-up world for us all,* Soil thought grimly.

"15m should be out by tomorrow," 69 whispered. She moved slow and her voice was a drowsy drawl, confirming Soil's impression that she was almost ripe, and the zombies had upped her painkillers so she didn't lose her mind before they harvested her.

"How'd you know that?" The three of them huddled together, like free teens sharing dirty secrets.

The girl pushed a mass of creepers away from her mouth, revealing her rotted tooth-stumps, before replying.

"The rumor is--Painfield's already found the culprit. It's 666--he infiltrated the camp a week ago, they caught him this time though. He's been secretly taken away for early harvesting."

"666 and the anti-vegan underground are just mythological scapegoats," Soil said. "Every time the zombies fuck up, they blame him/them so we don't think their security's slacking."

(The three womancows spoke with their mouths full. They kept their voices barely audible, indistinguishable above the sounds of their eating. 219 in particular had no desire to get noticed by the servers again.

Around them, zombies wheeled chopped-up human bodies from table to table, heaping food on trays. They paid the trio no notice.)

"Not so," 69 insisted, speaking around a mouthful of roast penis, cock broth spurting like semen overflow from the corners of her mouth. "If he's a myth, why isn't there ever any number 666 on the farm? There must be some truth in the rumor."

Soil had no reply to that. It *was* true-- there was neither a Soil nor Earth 666 on the farm. Both years she'd been here no one had ever had that number. And it was said to be the same on all the other zombie vegfarms as well.

219 voiced her thoughts. "Look, maybe the zombies do it to give us false hope of escape. You know, as long as we believe there's

a resistance movement outside working to free us, we're unlikely to revolt."

"Not so," 69 repeated, her voice slurred like she was dying a week ahead of her appointment in the slaughterhouse. "666 just has fantastic powers of escape, he's a Houdini superhero. No way are the zombies going to hold onto him, till he frees us all."

Confused by the implications of their discussion, Soil resumed eating her plate of human tripe.

# Chapter 3

## *Die-Namite*

15m wasn't released the next day either, or the day after. Nor on the day after that. The farm grapevine confirmed that everyone else on his work detail had been let go, but Warden Painfield still had him.

Soil resumed panicking. Once the zombies tortured 15 enough, he'd surely tell them he'd given her the multikey.

Then the slaughterers would come for her early.

She was getting the hell out of this hell before that happened.

\#

Soil needed supplies: Food and brains.

A supply of brains was essential for protection against zombies.

"Wanna fuck up a zombie? Hit 'em with die-namite!" the saying went.

All undead persons were allergic to meat. Soil had no idea why that was. Raw or cooked, human meat made zombies sick, an actuality nothing like what had been portrayed in pre-undead-holocaust screen flicks.

If human meat was poison to zombies, human brains were worse. Zombie flesh literally exploded on the slightest contact with brains.

They blew up, period.

So for Soil, the safest way to ensure that no one stopped her fleeing the farm was to find some brains.

With a stash of brains, Soil felt certain she could escape.

#

She quickly made another decision--to take 219 into her confidence. A two-person escape was more likely to succeed than if she attempted her breakout alone.

She cornered 219 in the cafeteria and dragged her out to a bench in full view of the farm walls and the vegans patrolling its top.

"Just shut up and look at this," she said when 219 began protesting about being dragged away from 'such delicious food.'

(219's recent exceptionally compliant behavior had Soil suspecting the zombies had upped her doses of medications to forestall a repeat outburst of the kind she'd recently had in the cafeteria.

She attributed her friend's survival purely to her fatness: The vegans were unlikely to waste the extra potatoes she was growing in her extra body expanse unless she really gave them cause to.)

With the patrolling zombies watching the pair of them disinterestedly, she got the multikey out of her cuntbag and put in 219's palm.

"It's the key the zombies are looking for."

She gave the guards on the wall a bold glance. Well out of range to clearly see what she was showing the other womancow, they paid her no notice.

She'd planned for as much: No one expects a transaction in stolen goods to occur in plain sight.

Then Warden Painfield's helicopter flew over the farm wall and all the undead guards turned their attention to observing her landing.

It took 219 a moment to understand what she was looking at. Then she looked like she'd whoop for joy.

"If you dare call any attention to us, I'll fucking kill your fat ass before the zombies do," Soil warned her.

219 nodded and calmed down. "15m really did steal it then."

Soil nodded. "I'm getting the hell out before he squeals to the warden he gave it to me." She looked 219 hard in the face. "I need a partner to do this right. You coming with me?"

The womancow smiled. "Count me in." Her smile faded. "We'll need brains," she said.

Her statement was punctuated by the sound of Warden Painfield's helicopter shutting off its engines.

"The bitch is back," Soil said with venom.

# Chapter 4

Soil had total amnesia concerning the circumstances of her capture by the zombies.

She'd simply woken up in a bed in a farm nursery doped out of her skull's ass. The number 15f had already been tattooed onto her forehead.

In retrospect, Soil had been grateful for the drugs the vegans had flooded her system with. Without them, she realized she'd have gone mad on her first sight of the potato seedling tendrils growing out of her skin like electrical wires.

Like every other humancow the vegans caught, once awake, she'd been stood upright and shackled hand and foot to a plastic pole with its tip stuck up her ass.

The pole and its chains were designed so the new humancow couldn't pull out the freshly planted seedlings before they'd formed their parasitic nerve connections with their host's body.

The 'asspole' restricted body movement to an absolute minimum.

Once the potatoes had rooted themselves into their host's nervous system, they could only be pulled to the accompaniment of pain similar to that of amputating a limb or pulling a tooth without anesthetic.

#

Soil had remained in the nursery for two weeks--all the while kept standing upright via the pole in her anus.

She wasn't the only one so impaled. The blood potato nursery was a huge chamber with thousands of asspoles. Their neatly arranged rows, each with a mancow or womancow forcibly seated painfully atop it, extended as far as the eye could make out.

No shit.

Once successfully implanted, all humancows remained impaled the entire duration of their stay in the nursery. The poles were hollow, so they shat down into them, and with their freshly-planted parasites leeching half the nutrients they consumed from their systems, they hardly shat at all.

It was also in this nursery period that the zombie doctors had doped Soil and converted her vagina into her cuntbag--she'd woken from the anesthetic to find she had a zippered cunt.

Before leaving the nursery, a female zombie nurse had handed out roll-up mirrors, tubes of lipstick, powder compacts, and leaf-green nail varnish to all the new womancows.

The nurse was short, and like all vegans, bald and scrawny. A large scar over her left ear marked where she'd had her brains vacuumed out before they went toxic on her.

Her facial skin stretched over her skull like old gift-wrap paper. Her teeth were yellow like those of a rat. Her eyes bulged like they were about exploding with pus.

"You ladies have all been fitted with cuntbags," she said, her voice sounding like she was being throttled. "There are no dressers on any of our farms. Inside yourselves is where you'll find your only privacy. Keep everything you value in your cuntbags from now on."

With that brief speech, their careers as plots of human farmland had begun. Along with a thousand others, five hundred each of male and female, Soil had been loaded aboard a truck and shipped to farm 642.

#

The primary problem with blood potato cultivation was the crop's growth period.

Blood potatoes took five years to mature. Once processed, each tuber provided a day's nourishment to the zombie eaters.

"The figures don't make good reading where the survival of humans is concerned," 15m had told Soil once. "It's as good as a total holocaust. Even really fat humans can only host a maximum of fifty blood potato tubers--if you want a healthy crop. Most of us only carry thirty, max. With fifty-two weeks in a year, this works out that the zombies are cultivating two humans for five years to feed one zombie for one year."

"That's absurd," Soil replied. "For that ratio to make any valid sense they need to have loads of vegfarms."

"They do. Thousands."

She shook her head. "Uh-uh. At that rate they'll kill everyone off in no time at all." Her brow wrinkled in thought. "How many vegans are there anyway?"

"Rumor says millions, though I doubt they really number more than a few hundred thousand.

"That few?  And we can't kick their undead butts to kingdom gone?"

15 said nothing.  His eyes, however, reflected his sharing her wish.

(Like Soil, 15 couldn't remember his life prior to being a humancow.  It angered him to no end, in that doped impotent humancow anger, that a freak accident of fate had both dumped him in vegan zombie hell and robbed him of the memories of life outside the farm, which would have been a major comfort.

The only info he'd been able to glean from the nursery nurses was that he'd been shot in the head by a romantic rival, and would have died had the vegan troops not arrived quickly on the scene to salvage him.

He had an ugly scar crater at the back of his head where the bullets had been dug out.

"Fifteen more minutes and you'd have been dead," his zombie informant told him, "you should be thankful."

15 would never be thankful for the remaining fifteen minutes, betraying his trust in time.

Most of his anger over his lost memories was due to the fact that now all his knowledge of the worlderness--the wastelands outside the farms--was of necessity second-hand info.

Soil was the only other humancow he'd met who had zero memories [drug-addled as they may be] of the worlderness.)

"I don't think the zombies give a shit about human conservation," he told Soil.

"But we're an irreplaceable resource," she countered. "Once they use up all available humans, they're fucked themselves."

"Not as totally as we'd love them to be. They won't die out or anything like that-- they're Necro's resurrected remember? All the blood potatoes do is keep them from drying up-- keep their corpses nice and supple. This farm and all the others are nothing more than sources of vegan health food."

The other thing potatoes did was 'animate' the undead. Through these dubious 'miracles' of modern nutritional science, zombies were no longer the shambling, bloodthirsty monsters of retro horror fiction.

Eating the parasitic legumes upped vegan reflexes to at least human levels, sometimes reputedly a lot more.

It was almost like blood potatoes were the non-sentient servants of the undead, leeching human vitality from their host's flesh and storing it for future zombie retrieval.

# Chapter 5

Warden Painfield was a pretty tall painfully-thin zombie woman, or xombina.

A mid-level bureaucrat, Painfield was also related by marriage to the DEZA, the Decadent European-Style Zombie Aristocracy.

The warden was an exceptionally fashionable woman. In addition to always being impeccably turned out, Painfield always carried about her zombie repair kit, a vanity case containing an assortment of glues, fillers, tapes, surgical staplers, and suturing needles and threads.

To Painfield, there was nothing worse than discovering you'd torn a strip of skin off, and lacking the requisite tools to put yourself back together again. Oh no, undead Humpty Dumpty.

Like all fashion-conscious DEZA females, Painfield had leaf-hair.

She'd had the expensive operation performed on her once her brain had decayed.

Rather than have the usual procedure of vacuuming out the decayed brain tissue and packing the empty space with plastic foam, Painfield had opted to have the entire top half of her skull removed, and her head filled with earth in which a Japanese bonsai tree was planted.

Careful maintenance of the tree's foliage provided Painfield and other high-class zombie ladies with lush leaf-hair.

#

Now Painfield crossed the lawn separating her helipad from the farm's slaughterhouse and power plant.

The issue of the missing multikey weighed heavily on her, not because she felt the humancows had it (or even had the presence of mind to do anything with it if they did--she kept them too heavily doped for them to exhibit that much independent thought), but because if news of its loss filtered outside the farm, it could prove embarrassing to her, could be interpreted as evidence she wasn't up to her assigned task.

Worse still, it would provide additional 'evidence' for the misogynists opposing the female domination of the agricultural sector of the vegan economy.

There were many envious of her position as warden, bored housewives mainly, who'd like nothing better than to pull the carpet out from beneath her feet and re-tile the floor with themselves.

Painfield understood how they felt. She'd been a bored housewife herself once, loved and pampered and with nothing worthwhile to do all day long except brood disgustedly on how she had nothing worthwhile to do all day long.

For a zombie, condemned to live forever in a half-rotted state (with most of their once-time human desires as dead as they themselves were), boredom was the most horrid thing imaginable.

From all accounts, possessing eternal life had been more fun in the old days, when all zombies did was stalk and eat the living (ugh--

the very thought of eating *meat* brought a spasm
of nausea to Painfield's vegan throat).

(A statistic: Eighty-six percent of
vegfarm wardens were previously bored DEZA
wives. Most had, like Painfield herself,
poisoned their husbands by feeding them meat and
taken over their jobs, simply to have something
creative to do.)

#

In the slaughterhouse, Painfield donned
protective clothing and conducted a perfunctory
inspection of the installation.

"I trust you had a pleasant trip in,
warden," Cutter, her head slaughterer said.

She grunted. "Nothing's pleasant till we
find the missing key, Cutter."

The zombie nodded. "None of the work
detail have it, madam. We've examined them all,
both inside and out."

Painfield nodded. This just confirmed
her suspicions.

She smiled. "Forget the damn key. It's
most likely sliding between the gears of some
piece of machinery. It'll make its presence
felt sooner or later by messing up the machinery
in question."

Cutter was visibly relieved by her stance
on the issue. "Do you wish to inspect the
slaughter room now warden?"

Painfield pulled the hood of her
protective suit over her hair-tree and fastened
it. Peering out the suit's face bubble, she
checked to ensure her gloves properly covered
her hands and nodded at Cutter.

"Yes, let's."

#

Painfield always found the certainty with which her slaughterers moved while killing humancows reassuring.

In this room, watching the steel conveyor ferry them in living, and moments later, away dead, reaffirmed to her the infallibility of natural process.

The worlderness outside could be a total fuck-up, but here, all was well with eternity.

The vegan race had food to eat for another day.

A metal trough on the floor traced the entire course of the conveyor belt through the room.

It was packed with shit, brown stinky turdboats floating in a urine ocean. Humancows always made a mess when they died. It was comical, the way they voided their waste at the moment of death--like they sought to cheat the cleaners in the butcher room of the pleasure of vacuuming the feces from their dead asses.

She walked along the conveyor belt with Cutter, running gloved fingers through cow foliage. All those she touched looked up at her through anesthetized eyes.

She expected they thought she was God.

The slaughterers backed respectfully away from the killing station at Painfield's approach.

Cutter primed a boltgun for her. She received it from him with a cold smile, savoring its balanced weight as it swung on its chain as much as she'd once savored her murdered husband's caress.

The conveyor moved. A womancow's head swung into place before the boltgun.

Painfield expertly placed the gun muzzle beside the ID number on the womancow's forehead. She pulled the trigger.

A sensual thrill raced through her as the eight-inch-long steel bolt punched its path through the cow's head.

Painfield tingled deliciously as the womancow corpse crapped and peed itself.

She became one with the boltgun, feeling an emotional connection to it--this instrument of mass death. She killed ten more humancows before feeling her tension over the missing multikey lift off her shoulders like a helicopter.

She handed the boltgun to Cutter, becoming once again brisk and businesslike.

She cursed herself for getting carried away by the pleasant process of administering death.

#

Warden Painfield regretted that she had no time today to watch the brain-scoop guillotine in action. As with the boltgun, she loved its mortal perfection, the flawless way it cut its preprogrammed route through each succeeding humancow head from temple to crown, afterwards scooping out the head's contents like a child would eat ice cream in ancient times.

As with every zombie, human brains terrified Painfield. Still she found the sight of them hard to resist, like a tractor beam magnetized her towards them.

She *loved* the deadly way they glistened when exposed in their skulls (like penis-heads peeking out of foreskins), how they looked like testes once the scoop had them in its nets, how they dripped cum-like fluid while their separate conveyor ferried them to the power plant, running parallel to the twin routes of corpses and shit.

Painfield relished her sex metaphors. Hardly anyone she knew fucked anymore. The feeling she got killing humancows was the closest she came now to eroticism.

Murdergasm. Not sex for sure, but the next best thing.

#

Painfield grudgingly left Cutter and the slaughterers.

Outside she stared for a while at the power plant, where human brains and excrement were mixed and enriched in reactors to critical concentration, then excreted in blocks used to power the vegan DEZA Empire.

Brainshit was also the modern gunpowder.

The sight of the reactor filled her with pride: Humancows were the backbone of the zombie empire and she was one of those entrusted with tending them, ensuring that the empire had both the power and food it required.

She ran a hand through her hair-tree foliage, patting down branches the slight breeze was ruffling.

With a pleased smile she spun on her heel and made her way to her office.

#

Painfield's smile dissolved when she saw the memo her secretary had left her.

Dr. October.

She'd forgotten he'd be visiting her today. A week from today was time to harvest the specials.

#

Dr. October had delivered the two 'specials' to Vegfarm 642 two years previously, part of a top secret DEZA project.

Painfield's husband had been farm warden then.

"I'm not permitted to explain what the project's about in the interim," he'd told Painfield on those occasions she'd asked (normally over dinner).

Dr. October was a pleasant zombie. Much like her dead husband, he made being undead seem that much less boring than normal.

"C'mon Doc, what kind of secret is it? It isn't like if you tell me you'll have to kill me--we're already dead!"

They'd shared a laugh at that.

"No no, can't tell. It's *really* classified. Other than the direct research team and the DEZA council, no one can have even the slightest inkling what we're doing." His gaze became serious. "It's in case it fails. If *that* were to happen, the disappointment, the dashed hopes would be... What I can tell you, is that if the project succeeds, its effect will be revolutionary to our vegan way of life."

He'd paused to take a bite of his potato.

It squirmed in semblance of life as he cut into it, its vegetable face registering pseudo-pain.

Painfield was amused by the tenacity with which blood potatoes clung on to their unlife.

Take for instance, the one on Dr. October's plate.

Though half-eaten, it stubbornly fought against the fork and knife which were the agents of its consumption, slapping its fibrous arms against the prodding metal. It had no intelligence, and yet resisted a death that in the cosmic scale of things meant less than its unlife.

She'd eaten some of her own lunch too, noting it had been very well processed. None of the many roots sticking out of its body showed any red spots, telltales of the nerve connections they'd had in their host's body.

"The council thinks highly of you, Painfield," Dr. October said around a mouthful of potato. "They're all highly impressed by how you've kept the farm running smoothly--even increased crop output--since your husband's unfortunate... death."

He put just enough stress on the last word for the emphasis to be ambiguous.

(Dr. October was no fool: He knew very well that the attractive xombina seated opposite him had poisoned her husband to inherit his job. The DEZA authorities overlooked too much, he felt. He intended keeping Warden Painfield as far from him as she currently was--at arm's length. Outside of work, he worked hard to have nothing to do with her other than work.

The success of project 15, however, necessitated that he keep the woman happy--an increasingly unpleasant task he was becoming increasingly expert at performing.)

Now he smiled his scholarly ghoul's smile. "How are my test subjects, by the way?"

Painfield shrugged. "So, so. Neither exhibits any exceptional behavior. If you ask me, I'd say your experiment's a failure." She noted his frown and quickly added: "Not that I've any idea what you're expecting of them of course."

She smiled innocently. "Except you think now's a good time to intimate me of your research."

Dr. October avoided the trap at the last moment. Damn! He really had to be careful with this xombina. He smiled in return. "Just be patient till harvest time, dear."

Painfield affected nonchalance. "Actually I'm keeping the male of your pair in custody at the moment."

Dr. October's ears pricked up. "15m? What happened?"

Painfield liked the worried look on his face. She wasn't stupid; she said nothing about the missing multikey.

"He's been getting erections. We'd like to know *why*."

Dr. October visibly relaxed at her words. Painfield smiled wickedly at the look of relief on his face.

She wondered what the fuss was over this pair of 15ses--they had to be something exceptional.

So far though, all she'd noticed was that 15m was largely immune to the drugs that effectively neutered all humancows.

(He also had very large--almost fist-sized--balls, which was unusual.)

Humancow sex--maybe that was the big *fucking* secret.

"The erections are nothing exceptional," the doctor said, in a tone that insisted they were *very* exceptional. "You must have noticed how enlarged his testicles are--all part of the experiment."

He stared hard at his companion, his gaze cutting her like a spear.

"I must request, no, insist, that you release 15m back into the herd."

Painfield shook her head. She was enjoying this--she liked the feeling of having the doctor's balls in her hand.

She squeezed them. Not too hard, mind, just enough to discomfit him.

"The problem is my security fear for my womancows. What if 15m *rapes* one of them?"

"That's impossible. 15m wouldn't... the experiment..." He realized he'd almost said too much again. "Well, warden, there's nothing problematic with your holding him in custody.

The safety of your herds must clearly be your primary concern, and in addition, the experiment will be over a week from today anyway. What *will* be very problematic for you..." he paused slightly to let the warning sink in, "... is any of your medical staff performing tests on him while in your custody." He smiled. "The council's tolerance only extends so far. One slip-up is often sufficient to bring one's buried corpses to the surface of one's graveyard."

He reached across the table and patted her hand. "I've seen bad things happen before to others less careful than yourself. I'd hate to see similar happen to you. I hope you understand me."

She smiled back, thin-lipped. The sweetly veiled rebuke/warning/threat left her mouth bitter. "I most certainly do, doctor."

They resumed their lunch.

#

Though Soil had no idea of it, this conversation between warden and doctor prevented Painfield from incarcerating her also on suspicion of collusion with her numbersake.

Dr. October's warning rang bells in Painfield's mind.

She resolved to have nothing further to do with his experiment.

To save face, however, less the doctor thought she could be pressurized, she'd leave 15m where he was. As of now he could fuck the leaves in his crotch all night long for all she cared.

# Chapter 6

## *We **need** brains*

There was a variation to Soil's 'last walk' dream now, one she'd begun dreaming the day 15m had given her the multikey.

In this new dream, everything proceeded the same up to the point at which her head was slit open by the guillotine and her brains scooped out, but now, rather than dump her corpse onto the conveyor that would take it away for processing, the slaughterers spread her legs wide...

They fucked her corpse, over and over again, fucked it while her empty decapitated head screamed and screamed in pain.

Screamed for Necro to deliver her.

*Necro?*

#

"We're getting no brains in there, that's for sure," 219 said. "What the hell made you suggest it?" Her voice still slurred slightly from drugs, but the unaccustomed adrenalin flooding her system from plotting their escape effectively throttled their effect.

Soil agreed with her. From their vantage point opposite the power plant they watched the heavily-armed zombie patrols.

"Let's get," 219 said.

They got.

"If we can't get brains from the power plant," Soil said, as they walked back, looking like two trees, "our only option left is the slaughterhouse."

She shrugged off 219's incredulous look. "It's never guarded."

"Only because it's *never* empty. What is *wrong* with you?"

What *was* wrong with her? Soil was pondering that question herself. Ever since she'd received the multikey from 15m, she'd started feeling nothing was impossible to her, that there were no longer any boundaries.

It wasn't a totally new feeling. Smothered by chemical layers of drug camouflage, she'd always sensed odd possibilities in herself.

Only until now there'd been nothing to focus her untapped reserves on. She'd been a scalar quantity--magnitude without direction. Now she had escape as her focus, she was close to becoming reckless. She had no idea either how far she'd go if they'd didn't get out soon.

And she wasn't the only one, 219 was in as bad condition as she. The womancow's leaf-framed face was flushed with excitement. The kindled hope of escape was burning through the drugs she was doped with like they were paper.

Sooner or later someone was going to notice the two of them weren't behaving normally.

They sat on a bench and watched the guards patrol the farm walls.

"We need brains," 219 said. "Without them, we've absolutely no chance of getting out of here."

"We already know that," Soil said. "Stop saying it."

Soil thought and thought and thought. Neuro-projectiles were required. She felt the fork of the catapults they'd made press against her bladder through her upper cuntbag wall. Useless bits of wood and rubber except...

"We'll have to kill someone," she decided.

219 looked at her and nodded. "I was thinking the same thing."

Soil nodded back. "Has to be someone who won't really mind."

"Wake up. *Someone who won't really mind?*"

Soil smiled. "69f for instance, she's scheduled to die day after tomorrow. We simply move the time forward by twelve hours."

Once she'd said it, she realized there was now no longer any chance of a retreat. She'd set their departure date.

219 nodded her agreement. "Best it's 69; she's already too far out of it to care anyway." She thought a moment, added: "You sure one head'll be enough? 540m's due to die same day. He's also in our dorm." She saw the disgusted look on Soil's face. "What I mean is--there're two of us right? So I keep one head of brains in my cuntbag, you keep the other, that way we can't run short."

Soil shook her head. "No space. I'll store the brains. You keep supplies in your cuntbag. We're raiding the cafeteria before leaving."

219 looked like arguing about having to stick meat up inside herself," so Soil added: "Not just for food--we'll need a meat cleaver to kill 69."

219 shrugged. "Okay, whatever you say. You're the boss."

## Got to Get-away

They waited till it was dark, dark, dark, before hitting the cafeteria.

It was deserted, except for a loudly snoring mancow sprawled atop a table.

They walked over and peered at his face to ensure he wasn't about sounding an alarm. The line of drool sluicing down his chin told them all they needed to know--that he'd be in the slaughterhouse maybe tomorrow. Soil bent closer, made out the number on his forehead.

"It's 540m," she said.

"I told you we should fucking kill him and 69."

Looking disgustedly down at the doped mancow, Soil decided 'why not?'.

They padded quietly back to the closest furnace pit.

"You'd think the zombies would be smarter, and not leave knives out in plain view," 219 said.

"They're already corpses--they're not scared of being attacked with knives," Soil reminded her. "Zombies only fear brains." She frowned grimly. "You also forget--we're meatfield beef--too anesthetized on painkillers to have initiative."

They took a meat cleaver each. Both already had their catapults slung around their necks.

They returned to the snoring 540m. Each looked at the other.

"How do we do this?" 219 asked.

"I've never killed anyone before either."

"Hit him hard across the middle of the face. That way we'll break out his brain as well."

Soil stepped back a bit, and lifted her cleaver well over her head.

She brought it down with all the force she could muster.

When the cleaver blade hit 540m, she felt a shockwave travel through her arm like she'd dislocated it. She dropped the meat cleaver, and gripped her arm, wincing both from the pain, and at the 'ping' the knife made hitting the ground.

"Wow," 219 said.

Soil looked. She saw she'd chopped the top of the mancow's head completely off. 540m was twitching like a worm. Blood spurted from his head.

They didn't bother waiting till he'd twitched to death. Soil bent over his corpse and dug her knife into the soft brain meat.

She cut it out of his skull in chunks, then both she and 219 wrapped the brains into little packages in leaves taken from the corpse and stuffed them into her cuntbag.

They kept the brains that had separated from 540's head with his skullcap for immediate use.

Soil paced impatiently while 219 stuffed her cuntbag full of livers, kidneys and hands.

She realized they'd both underestimated how much brains a human head contained. She was so stuffed with brains she felt like she was going to have a baby. No way was she going to be able to fit 69's brains in her cuntbag also.

219 walked back over. She was walking odd. Soil peered closer. Between the leaves obscuring her thighs, she saw toes. Shit, it was a foot--219 had stuffed a leg up between her own legs.

Soil shrugged. "I guess we got to eat on the way," she said.

219 nodded. "We go do 69 now?"

Soil grimaced. "Fuck 69. If I stuff another chunk of brains up inside me I'll blow up like a zombie." She pointed at 219's third leg. "And you look worse than I feel." She pointed at the east wall. "Let's just get the fuck out of here."

## *xcape*

The simplest way out of the farm was through the east wall (mainly because that was where all the farm vehicles were parked).

"Keep alert," Soil said, as they crossed the farm. They first crawled on hands and knees indistinguishable from lawn shrubs, then, once in tree shadow, regained their feet.

They walked as silently as they could, both holding their catapults at the ready, loaded with lethal lumps of brain matter. Being unable to hold both them and their catapults, they'd abandoned their meat cleavers.

There were no gates on this side of the farm, just a guard post--a single-story house built through the wall, so that it was half-in, half-out of the farm.

The post served a dual function, being both the receiving station for new farm intake, and also the route for shipping its potato crop out to the DEZA Empire.

Soil had chosen this way out because it was the least patrolled.

#

The 'unguarded' appearance of the east wall guard post was intentional, a vegan psychological tactic to depress meatfield spirits.

The strategic location of both the slaughterhouse and a power plant, along its approach, screamed the subliminal message at the farm residents:

'You are nothing more than a source of food and energy. It is your destiny--you can *never* be more than this, so don't trouble yourself with trying.'

Whatever small initiative still existed in a humancow's head after the copious drugging she or he received was intended to shrivel once the 'unguarded' guard post was considered.

It was simple reverse psychology: We leave this way unguarded because you are *unable* to flee.

The tactic worked. This was the first time in the farm's fifty-year existence that a humancow had EVER traced this path after dark.

#

"They don't think very highly of us," 219 said, as they navigated their way through the shadows. "There are no guards."

"They've no cause to think highly of us," Soil replied her. "We're less than meat."

"You don't think highly of us either," 219 said.

"There's little to think highly of," Soil retorted. "This way out's so open because they're certain of their hold over us. We're cows after all. None of us would dare attempt leaving the farm, even if the gates were open all day long."

True. Already, both womancows felt the oppressive weight of their years of emotional conditioning threatening to smother them. This couldn't be done, they couldn't escape, they couldn't...

Soil gasped at the choking emotional pressure. "We can't, we can't--"

"Shut up," 219 whispered. "You'll make them hear us."

Soil fell silent, let 219 lead the way.

They left the buildings behind them, sidled up toward the house in the wall.

"Shit," 219 said, as the night shadows thickened into the guard post. "We're actually going to do this. We're going to make it out of here alive."

"Shsssh, shut the fuck up!" Soil whispered. "Zombies."

Both hurriedly stuffed their mouths with brains.

#

Catapult strings stretched taut, cheeks bulging with brain chunks, both womancows advanced toward the guard post.

Four zombies sat around a table, talking. One had a blood potato in his mouth, its nerve tendrils wriggling like worms.

"Let's hit 'em." Soil and 219 let fly with their catapults.

Both brain projectiles hit the zombies in their faces. Both undead vegan heads exploded with that silent violence brains did to zombie tissue. There was a flash of light and some smoke.

The other two zombies stared perplexed at their dead colleagues, their headless bodies swaying in their seats, for a moment, then spun to face the window. Both lost their heads instantly to brain chunks hastily spat from cheeks and reloaded into catapults.

The two womancows cloistered themselves inside the guard post.

"This is too easy," 219 said.

"The zombies simply don't expect any of us to escape," Soil said. "I think all the humancows on the farm could walk out through this entrance, if we weren't so totally conditioned to being food growers."

The sparks from the exploding zombie heads had, however, been seen outside the guard post.

#

Soil noticed the approaching glows.

"Inside! Quick!"

They ducked through the doorway just before the wall floodlights arched over the post.

Soil pushed open the inner door. "We've the advantage that even if the zombies suspect a breakout attempt, they'll be so concerned about maintaining the mystique of this place they won't dare sound an alarm and wake the farm."

219 nodded. She looked from Soil to the quartet of headless zombies and shuddered. All four bodies jerked uncontrollably while groping the air like they were looking for their heads.

"There'll be more through there," she said.

"We'll just have to kick their asses too," Soil replied.

Catapults reloaded, they entered the inner room.

#

The post's middle room, its primary clerical/processing hall, was dark and empty of anything except clerk furniture. The wall separating it from the outer room was a single floor-to-ceiling slab of bulletproof glass with a single door through.

Through it they saw the outer room had six zombie guards in it. Through its open outer door they saw the night skies of freedom.

They made themselves small in the darkness.

"There's our transport," 219 whispered, indicating the outer room's left wall, against which four large hoverbikes were parked.

Soil looked at 219. "Safer to just run for it once we're outside."

"We'll get nowhere on foot with the zombies chasing us on bikes. And they've choppers too."

She smirked at the look on Soil's face. "Don't worry; controlling them's easier than taking a shit. You push the 'go' button and it flies, then you control direction with the steering. Push the handlebars forward to go faster, pull them back to slow down. Push 'go' again to stop--after the first push it becomes a stop button."

She saw Soil was still unconvinced. "Look, fuck it, okay? I'll drive. *What was that?*"

They listened. Footsteps were approaching outside the inner door.

"More guards," Soil whispered.

219 pulled back her catapult sling. "Let's hit them before they know what hit them."

"In or out?"

"What the hell d'you want to go back *in* for?"

They charged the zombies in the outer room.

# 

Half of the six zombies were headless before the other half realized what was going on.

The remaining three zombies' weaponry advantage over their attackers was neutralized by the disadvantage of disbelief.

The sheer unfathomableness of the idea that their cattle, mere meatfield animals, were attacking them, defeated them.

For these guards, the concept of superiority over their humancows didn't convert into practical experience.

Before they overcame their shock, they'd lost their heads as well.

Two 'died' by catapult.

219 smirked and approached the third, spitting a chunk of brains into her hand as she went.

Gun by his side, the zombie stood confused, staring in turn from her to his five headless companions, then at the door on the far side of the middle room, which a group of guards had just burst through.

The vegan got over his shock and both raised his gun to shoot 219 and opened his mouth to scream for help.

Soil batted the gun from his hand, her arm creepers swishing like she was in slow motion.

219 stuffed her hand's contents into the zombie's mouth. "Have some brains, asswipe.

Fresh from the head, just like great-grandma used to love."

She ducked as the vegan's head splattered all over Soil.

"Quit fucking your fat ass around, will you?" Soil growled. "Wake one of those bikes and let's go!"

219 dashed for the row of hoverbikes. The just-arrived zombie wall patrol, which had been watching them feed brains to the last zombie in disbelief, guessed their intent and rushed to stop them.

The bulletproof partition glass, however, meant that each zombie had to come through the door in plain view.

And one at a time.

After Soil hit the first one through with a faceful of brains, the rest watched helplessly from behind the glass wall, impotent spectators.

"I can't make the damn bikes start," 219 called over. "No keys."

Soil fiddled about in her cuntbag and found the multikey. She tossed it to 219. "Try this. Supposedly works on everything undead."

She quickly returned her attention to the zombies, before they got thoughts of rushing her.

The key worked. 219 activated a hoverbike and rode it across to her.

"Get on," she told Soil. "We're free."

They split.

# Chapter 7

"The worlderness looks different from how I remember it," Soil said, as the hoverbike sped, headlights off, along a dust-coated highway.

"What do you remember?"

"Cities. Many of them."

"DEZA? You were in the zombie strongholds?"

"What makes you say that?"

"The vegan towns--the only ones of any size there've ever been around here. Free humans stay as far from the zombies as they can. The nearest human stronghold is Avala, five hundred kilometres away."

"Avala? I don't remember that name."

Familiar with Soil's amnesia, 219 shut up, left her to her thoughts, and drove.

#

They started hearing helicopters. Choppers.

"Shit!" 219 spat, "*not so soon.*" She turned her head. "Hold on tight. I remember some ruins a short distance down the road. We'll get there before they get us for sure."

She pushed the handlebars as far forward as they'd go. The bike leapt like a horse and doubled its speed.

#

The helicopters came in view, horrid black elongated masses against the sky.

These military helicopters were 'choppers.' Each had four arms of zombie flesh grafted to its sides, each meat-hand gripping a monster meat cleaver. The four limbs were wired into the helicopter's central computer--a jacked-up human brain.

The cleavers slashed constantly at the ground as the choppers came on--the aircraft seemed to walk on them.

Spotlights played from their undersides over the cracked earth, searching for the pair.

They rode two hundred meters ahead of the beams, but the distance shortened each moment. Thankfully the hoverbike left no dust trail their pursuers could follow.

Then the ruins appeared out of the night, monster shadows out to eat them.

"Ignore the zombies, we're *there*," 219 called back at her pillion rider.

The spotlights streamed at them. 219 skipped her hoverbike over black flagstones and into the bowels of the ancient town of Texas.

## In a city blues

219 stopped the bike between two walls.

"We're free," she said.

"Dead as well," Soil said. "We're moving targets."

"Not if we can lose this shitty vegetation." She gripped a tendril between her fingers and jerked at it. "Shit!" she screeched a moment later.

"Forget that for now," Soil whispered. "If the spotlights pick us out, we won't live long enough to harvest ourselves."

A cleaver slammed down a short distance behind them, destroying a wall.

They looked back; saw the hovering biomechanical bulk, its cleavers glittering in the glare of its spotlights. Amazingly, its spotlights hadn't found them yet.

"Shit!" Soil yelped. "Fucking *GO!*"

The bike leapt forward. Behind it, helicopter-wielded blades chopped the ruins up like they were slabs of meat on a chopping block.

Then the firing started. Slugs chewed up the earth all around the fugitive womancows like they'd just entered the mouth of hell.

219 steered the hoverbike through a building doorway and parked it. She jumped off.

"If we don't defend ourselves, we'll die tonight!" she whispered. "Gimme some brains girl!"

Soil pulled two brain wraps from her cuntbag. She handed one to 219, but restrained her with a hand when she wanted to load her catapult.

"Don't," she said. "They're firing blind. They don't know for sure that we're here. It's a ploy to flush us out if we are." She pointed out a window. "Look, other choppers are searching elsewhere for us."

219 looked and saw distant spotlights gleaming off distant chopper cleavers.

"We just lay low and they'll leave," Soil said.

The chopper searching the Texan ruins turned away from their location. They watched its spotlights dwindle into distant needles of illumination.

Once it was too distant for the thrumming of its propellers to be heard, both womancows gave a simultaneous whoop of delight.

"We're free now!" Soil said. *"Really free!"*

Interlude

The worlderness was baked, caked, after-fallout earth.  It was a place of dangers, stranger even than the long-forgotten mutations created by the acid rains that had purged Earth of God's original creation.

Almost everyone agreed what existed now was Satan's version of what that creation should have looked like.  Horrors stacked atop each other like building blocks.

But some said even Satan was disgusted with the modern world.  By their accounts, he'd left Hell under his wife's governance and embarked on a quest to find God, so he could ask him what the hell he thought he was doing fucking everything up like this and abandoning it.

Mankind had always been God's joke, Satan noted before departing.  But now the joke had turned sour.  And he was once again being blamed.

There was no sympathy for the devil.  People blamed Satan anyway.  Better the devil you know than forces you can't even begin comprehending.  The modern world had to be Satan's fuck-up--how else could the undead, whose rightful place was in Hell, walk in plain daylight?

This was no idle claim.  The zombies had come from fucking Hell.  Though now firmly plugged with giant metal dildo starships, the cunt doors in the ground from which the undead had emerged were visible for all to see.

The zombies had blocked the cuntdoors themselves.  There were said to be things underground even they were scared of.

Who or what had reanimated the zombies was unknown. Satan was still everyone's best bet. Always best to blame the devil you know.

#

The necros, the worshippers of Necro, refuted all these beliefs of the origin of the worlderness.

This, the re-creation, they said, was the work of almighty Necro, the god imperfect.

Part Two:
The Man from Death Raft 4

# Chapter 1

"Eat zombies!" Priest screamed at the assembly in the huge temple hut.

"Eat and live forever!" they thundered back at him.

"Eat zombies!"

"Eat and live forever!"

Priest raised his hands to calm the worshippers. "We eat the undead to live forever in this world for no longer is there life after death."

"Death, Death, Death," the assembled necros hummed like well-oiled machines.

Priest smiled paternally at his congregation.

Bound together by belief rather than race or tribe, the necros were of necessity a motley crew. Wooly-haired Negros and Negritas worshipped alongside blond light-skinned persons and people of in-between shades of color. Slant- and oval-eyed children gaped at Priest, taking comfort from each other's horror of him.

The head necros was a short fat olive-skinned man. Like all priests he was bald, his head tattooed with black runes exalting Necro. He had a long plaited black beard. His eyes were small and black as coal. They glittered coldly in his round face.

His thick lips were permanently set in a horrible oily smile.

Like his congregation, he wore clothes tailored from zombie flesh, shredded in strips and woven/plaited into fabric.

The only exception was his cloak, made of unprocessed zombie skin. It was made of vegan faces, all still possessing toothed mouths that chewed the air and eyes that rolled in horror.

Impressive as shit.

Priest raised his hands again. The assembly fell silent.

"It is time for the feast," he said quietly.

His assistant priests now brought out the plates of blessing, trays heaped with pieces of purified zombie meat.

Priest blessed the holy meal, sprinkling it with salt. It was shared out to the congregation, while he intoned a litany from the Book of Undeath:

*"True worshippers in the bosom of Necro,*
*We eat the undead to live through them,*
*Are energized by their passage through*
*us,*
*Exalted by our digestion of them,*
*Purified by their becoming our*
*excrement."*

The congregation sang their reply:

*"Death in life in death,*
*Life in death in life.*
*Undead and living in the food cycle,*
*The decree of Necro,*
*Lord of the re-creation."*

Priest continued his recitation / incantation:

*"For Necro, unable to create man in his image,*
*Awoke the dead as zombie instead.*
*And he gave them to man for sustenance,*
*Even as he gave man to zombie for sustenance..."*

The ceremony was a long strenuous one. From somewhere far beyond himself, holy energies dripped from Priest's corpulent frame onto his listeners.

When finally the ceremony was done, and all the worshippers in the temple had eaten the undead feast, he collapsed into his chair wheezing, as drained as if he'd run a race.

# Chapter 2

## *Necroculture*

Necros culture revolved around their death rafts.

Death rafts were floating villages, resembling more than anything else constructs from ancient movies about life after the apocalypse.

The rafts were on average a hundred meters long and fifty meters wide.

Their flooring was earth overlaying a reinforced plastic/metal platform floated by stolen zombie antigravity engines. Their buildings were multi-sized huts built from bricks of zombie meat.

Each raft carried fifty or sixty living huts. In addition, it was equipped with artillery stations, stores and food processing huts, and a temple.

The necros nation comprised ninety-five death rafts in total. These prowled the worlderness in widely dispersed groups of fours or sixes, a splitting for protection against zombie attacks.

The rafts in each group watched over each other, and assisted themselves to attack and defend against enemies.

Similarly the groups watched over each other.

The only raft excepted from groupings was Death Raft 4, Priest's raft, considered the center of the necros empire and the temple throne of Neck, God in flesh.

Raft 4 needed no protection of groups. The flagship of the necros empire floated in solitude over the baked earth, raiding also in solitude.

Necro's grace was sufficient.

And if the god fell asleep and his temple was attacked, then those death rafts nearest to raft 4 would join the fight and deal with the attackers. Necro had obviously fated them to be in the right place at the right time, because he was tired.

But there would be no fixed guard for Death Raft 4.

Never would the true believers let it be claimed by the zombie heretics that Necro was incapable of protecting those who trusted in him.

## Able Kane and Morphia

While zombies wore tailored human-style clothes, the necros used zombies for everything. Food, clothing, shelter... and sex.

Able thought of each necros death raft as a zombie processing station.

"I find it delightfully ironic," Morphia said as they watched a cargo of netted zombies swing over the prow of the death raft, peering through the net holes in stupefaction at being trapped by 'cows,' "the totally useless undead enter here and we make them useful."

She licked her lower lip. "As Priest says--'It's the Primary Truth in this new creation, zombies were created to provide man with everything we need'."

Able glanced at her out the corner of his eye. From sharing his hidden cynicism with religion, she mentioned Priest constantly now.

It had become irritating.

Morphia was beautiful and willowy. She was bald, her necros scalp-tattoos visible. Morphia was an assassin, her scalp runes spoke of violent death.

Morphia was also overall head of the necros military.

Like Able Kane and all other necros aboard the death raft, she wore a shirt and trousers of pleated zombie-skin fabric.

Able Kane, Morphia's lover, was tall and thin, with short black hair, a goatee, and a permanently distracted look in his eyes.

#

Morphia leading, they walked over to view the captured zombies up close. The netted undead were a mixed bunch of 'old' and 'young' in differing stages of potato-arrested decay.

Able Kane stared at a zombie girl who'd once been very pretty. Her face was stitched to her skull with metal thread, and she had a well groomed tree fashionably planted in her skull. The tree marked her as being a highbred rich-zombie, maybe even DEZA. She was dressed in ripped rose-colored fabric.

She saw him staring at her and spat at him.

Able was struck by an idea.

"This one," he whispered to Morphia, "I'd like her for our harem."

Morphia turned to look at the zombie girl. She nodded disinterestedly. "She tickles your fancy? I'll have her taken to our hut."

That settled it for Able. Morphia not being jealous at his requesting the xombina meant something romantic was up with her somewhere else.

The zombie girl had overheard them. Rather than be grateful she was being spared, she spat at Able again. He kicked her through the net. "Stop that, or it's the kitchen for you."

She didn't spit again.

#

The necros were first to admit they lived parasitically on the zombies--without zombiekind there was no necros culture, period. But so, it was decreed in the Book of Undeath.

All around the hovering rafts, buildings sputtered like funeral pyres.

Groups of necros walked between the fired buildings collecting still-twitching undead limbs and torsos, exploded off their owners by brain bullets, into sacks.

Morphia looked across the zombie settlement, to where another group was busy stripping the settlement's power plant. Once done dismantling the reactor technology, they'd drain off its precious brainshit mixture through metal hoses into the death raft's fuel tanks.

Morphia left Able to give orders to a group of soldiers.

"It's done," she said on returning to his side.

"Huh?"

"Bug eyes with the tits--she's yours." She still spoke with unstudied indifference.

*Oh Fuck,* Able thought, watching the xombina being led off for purging from blood potato poisons, *this is worse than I imagined.*

The girl turned to glare at Able, like confirming his bad thoughts.

#

The zombies were separated into groups. Most (particularly the 'aged'--a zombie category Able found amusing--how could someone be both dead/undead and 'aged'?) for processing for food; others (particularly 'kid zombies' who had relatively supple flesh) for processing into clothing. A few were kept as slave labor.

The most attractive--least decayed-- zombies, both male and female, were reserved as sex toys.

The zombies went quietly where they were led, into the marked pens that signaled their respective fates.

"We need to leave here fast," Able said. "Won't be long before choppers arrive from Vega."

Morphia ran a finger over her shaven head, licked her lips.

She laughed. "Only if they get a distress call, which we made sure they won't. Still you're right that we need to leave." She stopped a soldier returning from herding the zombies into their pens. "Hurry up the collectors," she told him. "We've a human village to hit before midnight."

They watched the brainshit pump being wheeled out to the stripped power plant. Once it began humming, they walked to their hut.

#

Their hut was large. It was partitioned into standard necros quarters--bedroom, living room cum toilet/bathroom, Able's library/lab, and the shrine, which neither of them ever used.

Until now.

"I want to pray," Morphia said once the vertical strips of zombie flesh forming the door swished shut behind them. "I need spiritual cleansing before the next raid."

Able looked at her askance. "Pray? *You?* To whom?"

She smiled. "To Necro, of course." She patted his cheek. "Don't get lonely, darling, Bug Eyes will be here shortly if you feel like relieving yourself."

She stripped off and vanished through the meat strip door to the shrine.

Able Kane sat and pondered.

Morphia's suddenly acquiring religion...

#

Able Kane was head necros food technician--head of necros food research. His job was maintaining the standards of meals for the tribe.

(As a personal task, Able had also set himself the puzzle of finding a way to shorten the de-poisoning period for zombie meat.)

In the ultimate nutritional/biological irony, zombie flesh was as toxic to humans as human flesh was to zombies.

Zombies, however, had blood potatoes, and lacked a religion which insisted they feed directly on their adversary.

The necros religion insisted that its adherents do so.

Without eating their gods for breakfast, lunch and dinner, the necros were less than they should be.

So food scientists were the foundation of the otherwise unscientific necros culture.

The present method of detoxifying/'purifying' zombie meat was by soaking it in large tanks of menstrual blood collected using sponge rats.

Sponge rats looked like the household pests of ancient times, but their flesh was super-absorbent tissue designed to suck and retain moisture from the arid worlderness air and soil. To better facilitate their water-retention capability, their bones were hollow storage reservoirs.

A bowl of water poured on a sponge rat would all be sucked in through its skin pores, with little attendant increase in its size. The same result would be obtained upon dropping the rat into the bowl of water: It would mop all the liquid up like a sponge, hence their name.

The water could be retrieved by squeezing the rats.

Sponge rats absorbed blood just as efficiently as they did water, so necros women used them as tampons, inserting them alive into their vaginas during their periods.

Once soaked full of menstrual blood, the rats were pulled out by the tail and dropped into the food-purification tanks, along with zombie meat.

The rat corpses rotted, releasing both the blood and enzymes that stimulated the blood to stick to the meat and draw its poisons from it.

It was an effective and efficient system, one that saved both menstruating women and food technicians a lot of bother.

#

"There *must* be a simpler way to do it," Able often told Morphia.

"We don't <u>need</u> a simpler way," she always replied. "There's no shortage of zombies to catch and eat, or of *bleeding* women to purify them either. And using the rats is nice and clean."

"I'm not talking about the mode of collecting the blood," Able explained. "I mean...four days to purify each batch is simply *too long*. Just imagine if we could have zombies caught at dinnertime ready for breakfast the next morning."

"I still don't see the need for it," Morphia said. "You're already eternally far ahead with food production. You've got it so worked out..." She leaned over and kissed him. "You worry too much, Able, and it worries *me*..."

Able looked into her eyes and found solace in the fact that she loved him. "I can't help but worry," he said. "Providing food for an entire tribe is a monstrous responsibility. Just imagine what would happen if we lost our stored food stock."

"Or if our women suddenly all hit menopause at the same time." She laughed. "Able, darling, it can't happen."

Able laughed with her. "Still you can't but admit it would be nice to see a zombie you fancied for supper and simply be able to slice off some meat and roast it."

"If that's what you have in mind, it makes more sense to alter us necros, so we can eat zombies raw."

They'd laughed at that, then retired for sex.

That conversation had set Able thinking.

Despite his joking with Morphia on the matter, Able Kane could never relax, could never believe the necros' current food processing system was disaster-proof. And it was his responsibility to ensure that it was.

Morphia's joke about altering human metabolism to eat raw zombie flesh stuck with him and altered the direction of his research.

And while futilely seeking to alter human metabolism, Able Kane discovered something he'd definitely *not* been looking for.

Something earth-shattering that he intended not mentioning to anyone. EVER.

# Chapter 3

## *Able's Lemonhead Xombina*

Caught between his research troubles and his newfound romantic misery, Able suddenly felt extremely depressed. Before he could savor his misery, however, he was provided with a distraction.

The door strips fluttered.

The zombie girl entered. Able dismissed her two escorts and walked her through into the bedroom. She followed meekly, walking like she was dreaming. He fastened the chain around her neck to a metal ring in the wall and sat on the bed facing her.

"Whatever you do," he said, "don't you *dare* spit here. Ensure you remain constantly grateful to me that you're not food."

She nodded back at him dreamily, already deep in withdrawal from blood potatoes. "Yesss, Masssterr!" she mumbled. Her eyes were now swollen like they'd burst. Zombie cold turkey was never fun to watch.

(The necros medics had sped up her regression with an enzyme shot that accelerated zombie potato metabolism. She now had as little intelligence/initiative as an ancient zombie-movie zombie.)

Able smirked. Zombies were less than shit. The absolute nadir of Necro's creation, not its acme, like Priest claimed. Utter garbage. Fucking trash.

"Not so tough now, are you, without your damn vegetables?" He spat in the girl's face.

The spit dripped down her nose and ran over her lips.

"Take off your clothes."

He watched her strip off her rose-colored dress. Her body was bony but good, her dead skin taut over her ribs. She had few wounds and wasn't maggoty. Her ass was okay, and like Morphia had remarked, her withered breasts were big.

He nodded his approval. She'd do for a fuck-toy while Morphia fucked with his emotions.

He pulled her down on the bed. Her neck chain easily reached there from its wall fixing.

He loosened his trousers, then got a condom-worm from a jar on the dresser.

He spread the worm's jaws and pulled it on over his cock till it was nice and taut. He winced with the pain of it sinking its fangs into the root of his member to anchor itself.

He waved to his new undead concubine.

"Spread your legs nice and wide zombie girl. Time you learn your new role in existence."

"Yessss, Massssterrr!"

Able climbed on the bed and inserted his cock in her. For the first time he caught the smell of her head-tree. It was lemon.

## In the holy hut

Priest looked over the two xombinas the guards had brought to him. Both were youngish and relatively undecayed, clearly Morphia had reserved them for him.

Both swayed in their doped daze like old-time movie zombies.

Priest pried one of the xombinas mouths open, examined her teeth. Most were in good condition. He stuck a hand between her legs, wiggled two fingers in her sex.

The fingers came away maggoty, but there was no pus smear, the sign she was rotting.

He ate the writhing larvae and sniffed his fingers. She smelled moldy. It was a pleasant smell to Priest. A turn-on.

He examined the second undead girl, confirmed she was also in good condition.

He nodded at the guards, dismissing them.

#

When they'd left, he led the new additions to his harem into his bedroom.

There were four other xombinas in the bedroom; three were chained to the walls, and lay on zombie-skin rugs, their limbs languid, their eyes dull.

Priest's bed was a wide four-legged tub filled with maggots writhing over rotting meat. The fourth xombina in the room, Neck, lay on this bed of putrescent flesh, propped up on a half-decayed human torso.

Neck was a rarity--a zombie hermaphrodite. She was shapely and had thick white hair reaching to her waist. None of Neck's flesh withered--she existed permanently in 'rotting-corpse' condition.

Like Able's xombina, she'd once been pretty. Now, with her body decorated with rotting holes (in some of which maggots writhed) she was obscenely *impressive*.

Neck's left cheek was a gangrene-rimmed hole through which her teeth were visible.

She complemented perfectly the obscene bed she lay in.

Neck was Priest's wife and was believed by the necros to be the living incarnation of their god Necro. Was God in Flesh. Priest fucked her for spiritual rejuvenation.

(Once a year, at the Festival of Undeath, Neck fucked Priest publicly, her maggot ejaculations over his fat ass clear signs that the god Necro approved of his worshippers.)

Neck had been in Priest's holy hut for six years now.

Priest left her unchained. Neck had no intentions of escaping--here she was in a position of power. It was intoxicating to be regarded as deity.

(Unlike other zombies, Neck showed no withdrawal symptoms from blood potatoes, neither in her reflexes or her mental capacities. In addition, she ate human meat, purified by being soaked in a tub of human urine and maggots--the bed she shared with Priest.

She also wasn't allergic to brains.

Except for her special appearances in the temple, Neck was never seen in public. It was a capital offense to view her unsummoned.)

"Welcome home, Priest," Neck said. Dripping white larvae, she climbed off the bed and helped Priest chain the two new xombinas to the wall. "How was the temple worship?"

He picked maggots from her hair and chewed them absentmindedly while replying. "Able Kane wasn't there again."

"He never is--you must stop letting it get to you."

"It rankles for one so exalted to be so unfaithful."

They finished securing the zombie girls. Neck disrobed Priest and hung his cloak of faces on a frame scarecrow designed for it. They sat on the bed.

She took Priest's fat hands in her slim ones. She loved the head necros for the power he afforded her. "It's good for us... you to be seen to tolerate Able."

"But how long? Morphia tells me he constantly speaks of altering our way of life. The man is danger personified."

(Priest spoke from his heart. It pained him greatly that in this world where the super-creation, the zombies, had abandoned worshipping their own god Necro [and had abandoned his demand that they eat human flesh], that even his true worshippers, the necros, were being found wanting.)

Neck sat back, her huge eyes gleaming. Priest mentioned Morphia too often for her liking nowadays.

She snorted. "Morphia? Another heretic; no better than her lover." She placed her right hand in Priest's lap, fondled his cock through his pants. "A pity they're both indispensable to our way of life," she sniggered.

Priest pushed her fondling hand away. "Not now, the worship drained my energies." He got what Neck was getting at. "Morphia is indispensable--she heads our army. Able Kane on the other hand, isn't--all he does is whine about the quality of our meat and cutting down purifying time. Any of his assistants, even you or I, can do his job--the process is already perfected."

Neck hid her displeasure at his rejection of her advances. "You believe it's time we dispose of Able Kane?" she asked calmly.

Priest nodded grimly at her. "We've tolerated his mental poisons long enough. I think it's time our head food technician entered your meat bed for purification."

"Okay," Neck agreed, "but we need the pretext of an excuse. Why not get him to admit he's a heretic?"

Priest smiled, impressed by her wisdom. Morphia would soon be his. He took Neck's hand and replaced it in his crotch, letting her resume fondling him.

Neck smiled. She freed Priest's cock from his pants. Like himself, it was short and fat. Naked, Priest and his penis both looked like butt-plugs.

Neck already had a hard-on. Her cock was small but perfectly formed. Priest liked the fact that he could get all of it, including both her balls, into his mouth at once.

Neck dipped her right hand in their charnel-bed, jerked it free full of maggoty meat. She placed the decaying flesh and larvae over Priest's penis, and jerked him off with it.

Priest groaned. When unable to stand the pleasure any longer, he rolled his god over on her belly and inserted himself into her ass.

Unlike other necros, he never used protection--it would be an insult to Neck's divinity.

The violence of his thrusts into her ass sank them deep into their putrescent bed. Rotting meat and bones covered them like blankets.

While he fucked Neck, Priest licked her rotting wounds, licked her tongue through the hole in her face. Occasionally he ate handfuls of the maggots crawling over them both, and fed her with them also.

Their harem watched them screw with empty eyes.

# Chapter 4

Once Able Kane ejaculated, he felt much better.

It had been a long time since he'd fucked a zombie. Morphia's jealousy prevented them having any kind of harem. She didn't even want male zombies for her own use.

Able had forgotten the pleasure of a zombie body lying passive beneath him, waiting for him to do whatever he liked with it.

The xombina had hardly moved during his assault on her sex. Now she moaned like he'd hurt her. The lemon smell of her head-tree tickled his nostrils.

Able smirked at her. Zombies weren't shit; they were just refuse God had left out for necros collection.

Carefully unrooting its fangs from his flesh, he pulled the condom-worm off his penis and dropped it back into the jar on the dresser. It burped contentedly, swollen to twice its size, gorged on blood and cum.

Able left the xombina on the bed and pulled on his clothes. Then he went into his laboratory. Morphia's solemn intonations filtered through the zombie-meat walls; incantations strengthening her for the attack on the human settlement.

Now certain he'd not be disturbed, Able folded back several of the zombie-flesh squares carpeting the lab floor to reveal a trapdoor. Opening this exposed a rectangular hole he'd excavated in the earth over the raft's skeleton. Along with some papers and equipment, the hole contained a black box and a number of withered human arms.

Able carefully brought out the box and opened it. It contained a bottle of pink liquid--his discovery.

He stared, mesmerized at the bottle's contents, ethically transfixed by the implications of its existence.

Priest would kill Able if he knew what he held in his hands. It would change the world forever if it was ever used.

Able sighed, his depression returned. It never would be--it was too dangerous.

He shut the box and returned it to its hiding place.

#

Morphia emerged from the shrine and entered their bedroom.

She smirked at the xombina's disheveled state. She looked like a shirt someone had carelessly thrown on the bed.

"Take good care of him, veggie bitch," she said. "He's all yours."

"Yesssss, Masssterrrr!" the xombina hissed piteously.

Morphia laughed. Then she forgot her and began readying herself for battle.

She had no more time for Able Kane and his mad ramblings. Priest had opened her eyes to the sort of idiot he was.

# Chapter 5

The huge death-rafts floated silently into place around the human settlement of Dutchi and disgorged necros like plagues of soldier ants.

The raid was as quick and violent as a botched abortion. Within an hour of its starting, the village was destroyed and ranks of prisoners stood alongside the necros vehicle.

Accompanied by guards, Morphia walked through the ranks of captives. Occasionally, when they came to either a man of exceptional build or woman of exceptional beauty, she nodded. Guards pulled that individual out of line and forced them aboard the raft.

Everyone else, children inclusive, was converted to munitions.

They were decapitated, their heads split open like nuts, and their brains scooped out. The brains were piled high in metal tubs and loaded aboard the death raft.

Morphia nodded her approval.

She walked over to her selected captives, all staring horrified at the brains of their loved ones.

"You're lucky," she said, running a hand over her tattooed scalp. "You too will be necros like me." She smiled grimly. "If you are strong enough."

She stuck a knife into the breast of one of the male captives and twisted it. His face distorted with pain, but he made no sound.

Morphia nodded. "Good. You understand. Purification is the pain of your becoming someone from no one, something from nothing."

She pulled the knife out, stepped back to face all the captives. "At the moment you are all lower than my excrement. I would not permit you to lick my anus clean after I shit--you would defile it with your heresy. Each of you will prove yourselves worthy to worship Necro as he demands, or..." She pointed to the tubs of brains.

She left the shivering captives, and walked over to inspect the haul of brains in detail.

# Chapter 6

Morning came, and with it came trouble.

Not required for the night's raid, Able Kane had slept through it. Returning from lab to bedroom and finding Morphia gone, he'd fucked his new xombina concubine again, then fallen asleep beside her.

Now he felt VERY refreshed. He fried zombie sausages and eyes for breakfast, then got ready for work at the purification hut.

#

He was leaving the hut when the four priests arrived.

The priests were tall wiry men with plaited beards and shaven heads tattooed with hymns of praise to Necro. They wore sleeveless tops over ankle-length zombie-plait skirts.

Their leader carried a ceremonial staff of woven zombie bones topped with a baby's skull.

"Necro blesses you," he greeted Able amiably.

Able returned the greeting, bowing politely. "Morphia's not here," he said, "she hasn't--"

"You are doubly blessed," the lead priest said. "God and her priest request your immediate attention in the holy hut. You must accompany us to her presence now."

*Holy zombie shit,* Able thought, reading a threat into the request, even though the priests were unarmed. What now? He'd never been summoned to a private audience with Neck before.

#

Being in God's presence had the intended effect on Able Kane.

Standing in Priest's bedroom, staring at Neck on her bed of rotting meat, maggots squirming up and down the hermaphrodite's cleavage, was too much for his atheism to bear.

Her cock floated on suppurating tripe, its head nestled in an end of severed colon.

Able Kane had no sexual interest in penises not his own. Still, Neck stirred him sexually, her nakedness amidst the glorious putrid gore affecting him much deeper than his balls.

The concubines chained to the walls increased his sense of being in Haeven.

Hating his weakness, Able felt his faith in zombie rejuvenate itself.

"Come sit beside me, Able," Neck said, patting the bed.

He shambled over and sat beside her. The room's charnel house stink filled his nostrils like liquid perfume, forcing his belief in undeath as life's divinely decreed superior.

It was hypnosis beyond belief.

Priest entered then and sat facing them on the back of a xombina on all fours.

"Tell me your trust in I, the physical incarnation of Necro," Neck said. She laughed. "Not your true faith of now, but all you have believed of me before this moment, when you know me in truth as your truth."

A lamb placing the slaughter knife to its own throat, Able began speaking.

#

"You're not a novice Able Kane, you know the scriptures," Priest said silkily, intruding into Able's vision of Haeven. "In the new beginning Necro, unable to recreate heaven and earth, made the best of the mess he'd been left with.

"Unable to create a new man, he recycled the dead into zombie.

"Unable to create animals for food he decided they were unimportant, and decreed the food cycle--that zombie eat man and man eat zombie.

"But the undead angel Hereticos taught the zombie that meat was evil and they were deceived. They abandoned the truth and became vegan."

"I disagree, Priest," Able interrupted in a loud murmur. "Zombie meat is poison to us, as ours is to them."

Priest raised an eyebrow. "Only because zombie belief in Hereticos has made all existence unclean. But from the re-creation it was not so." He paused. "So we purify the vegan meat, purge it of evil. The zombie too are meant to purge human meat similarly and feed on it, to complete the food cycle. But they have abandoned the true worship of Necro for blood potatoes, the creation of Hereticos."

He held up an imperious hand to forestall Able's speaking. "And what is the result? Soon Earth will be empty--their unnatural actions kill off all humans."

"You lie," Able muttered. "You lie."

Neck spoke. "The vegan DEZA have abandoned the truth of the faith. In a year, at most, they will have killed off all edible humans on the planet."

Able nodded at the personification of God in flesh, the divine haze and the command he'd been given, forcing him to go on speaking things better left unsaid. "Impossible. You lie also."

"It is true."

"No, you lie."

Priest stared at him in horror. "You accuse *God* of lying?"

Able ignored him. He stared pointedly at Neck.

"I am a scientist--a man of reason, not faith. Are you certain of your figures?"

Neck nodded, concealing her gross distaste of him with a smile. "Certain enough. Soon only necros and vegans will be left alive. We patiently wait to convert them back to the true faith."

"We must turn the tide. Save our fellow humans," Able said weakly, unaware of his words.

"You wish to preserve excrement?" Priest asked dismissively. He'd concluded Able as beyond salvation, an abomination to be disposed of as fast as possible. "All who refuse to worship Necro and eat zombies are shit. They *must* become extinct--the re-creation holds no place for them."

Neck smiled, showing perfect teeth. "You must agree Able that it is ironic, but fitting, that the heretics kill themselves off. When there are no longer human meatfields for the vegan undead to grow blood potatoes in, they will return to the worship of I, the one true god."

"No," Able said, "I will save mankind."

"Necro will be revered by all," Priest intoned.

"Yes, by all," Neck concurred, staring pointedly at Able Kane.

"No," Able Kane repeated. *"Necro be damned.* Human salvation *is* possible, I can save them. I will be their messiah, lead them into the blessed dawn."

"Wait outside in the living room," Neck ordered Able. He staggered off, but turned back at the door. "I *can* save them," he repeated. "I have discovered a cure--no more will blood potatoes grow in human soil." He exited the room.

Once the zombie-flesh strips swished closed behind him, Neck frowned at her husband. "He is worse than I thought. Totally deluded. What more proof do we need of his heresy?"

She spat on the bed, then plucked an eye from a skull and sucked on it to calm herself. "It was all I could do to keep from strangling the idiot."

"Do not soil your divine hands," Priest said. "I'll have Morphia execute him immediately."

He called out of concealment the pair of under-priests he'd hidden to witness Able's heresies and sent them to get Morphia. They ran off, horrified by the blasphemies they'd heard.

Able's words about 'finding a cure' rang distress bells in Priest's mind.

He decided it would be best to demolish the heretic's hut in order to destroy any crap research Able had come up with. Even the dead could be dangerous sometimes.

#

The divine fog cleared from Able's mind in time for him to see Morphia enter, flanked by a pair of soldiers.

She'd come immediately. Both priests who'd summoned her away from overseeing munitions preparation had been in shock. They'd simply told her God needed her and staggered out of the weapons factory.

She'd left them retching beside it.

She bowed to Priest, now seated opposite Able in the living room, like they'd been having a pleasant conversation. "You called, lord?"

Priest pointed at Able. "Execute this heretic and make him part of God's meat bed."

Able stared blankly, his vision of zombie heaven not yet dissolved enough for him to know how much trouble he was in. He wished he could lie in Neck's arms while she tenderly feed him maggots from her belly.

Morphia frowned. This was too sudden. *Able, you total shit, what the hell did you say?* "Heresy, my lord?"

"Of the worst sort. We have witnesses to--"

The rest of his sentence was obliterated in the explosion that blew in one wall of the hut. Both Priest and Able were knocked off their chairs by chunks of zombie-wall. Able was knocked half senseless.

Morphia and the soldiers were flattened into the opposite wall. They peeled themselves out of the zombie-flesh masonry wincing, leaving body indents in the wall.

"It's a vegan attack!" Morphia growled. As confirmation, another two explosions rocked the death raft, though not near enough to damage the hut further.

Priest staggered to his feet, then dashed inside his bedroom. He returned a moment later. "God is unharmed," he panted. "We must protect her, first and foremost, and then fight the zombie heretics."

His voice shook with horror at the thought of harm coming to his divine wife.

He looked at Able, saw he was stunned, his eyes glazed, and forgot him.

"The divine one will be safe submerged within her meat-bed," Morphia said. "She doesn't breathe air. The meat covering will cushion her from shock and also prevent projectiles reaching her." The holy hut rocked again. "My soldiers will assist you, I must coordinate our defense."

Priest nodded.

Morphia exited the hut into a nightmare. Huge vegan choppers filled the morning air, hacking indiscriminately at huts.

She immediately realized this was a random raid--not a reprisal for their destroying last night's zombie settlement--the large dragnets trawling from several helicopters marked this as a livestock gathering expedition.

Righteous indignation flooded Morphia.

Stupid zombie heretics! The vegetable-eating undead bastards would <u>pay</u> for this!

She set off running for the nearest brain-cannon station. Then she remembered Able and stopped. She had no doubt the asshole prick had said whatever Priest had been accusing him of, and deserved to be chopped into meat for their god's sustenance.

But... She groaned. She couldn't just let Able die. They'd been *Lovers* dammit!

Cursing her weakness, she headed back towards the holy hut.

#

While explosions rippled the death raft, Priest and the two soldiers secured Neck in the bed.

They quickly dug a trench in the meat and maggots and submerged her in it. Then they piled the excavated meat over her.

As extra protective padding for Neck, they submerged Priest's entire harem also into the bed.

#

After ensuring first that Priest and the soldiers were out of sight, Morphia re-entered the holy hut. She dragged the stunned Able outside and some distance away, then pointed out across the raft, out into the worlderness.

Able stared at her like an idiot. She slapped him hard. His eyes swam into focus. She waited impatiently, until she was certain he understood her, before speaking:

"This is the only chance you'll have to escape becoming God's food," she told him. "You'd better get lost."

Leaving Able to figure out <u>how</u> to get lost, Morphia dashed off to command her troops in repulsing the attackers.

# Chapter 7

The sky thronged with huge biomechanical craft questing for live prey. Brainshit bombs poured from rear-situated hatches in each chopper's fuselage like they were crapping, whilst their immense cleavers laid waste to huts right and left in their quest to scare the necros out of hiding.

A number of choppers already had full nets of people. These hovered beside the death raft, avoiding the conflict.

By now sufficient necros troops had re-gathered their wits about them to mount a counter attack. Brain-cannons boomed like thunder around the death raft. Two choppers were simultaneously hit by brain shells penetrating their front windshields. Seconds later, assorted chunks of zombie flesh exploded out through all their windows.

With no pilots, both helicopters crashed into each other, painting the mid-morning sky with a black/orange explosion that became a rain of blast-distorted biometal chunks.

On ground and on rooftop, necros gunmen fired brain bullets at the biomech vehicles.

*Fucking zombie rain,* Morphia thought. *You wanna fuck with us, damn veggies? We'll teach you to fuck with us! Bring it, bitches!*

She reached the nearest brain-cannon assemblage. Its gunner was dead, his chest pierced through by a jagged metal spear.

She pulled the body out of the seat and climbed up into it.

"Eat brains, motherfuckers!" she screamed at the choppers as she began firing, stamping the cannon's reload pedal violently in between shots.

Brain shells were foot-long alloy canisters packed with a neural tissue payload wrapped around an explosive charge. On detonation, the shell splattered brains in a fifty feet radius. There was no escape for zombies trapped in the packed confines of a helicopter.

Protective clothing was of little use: A brain-shell's alloy canister was designed to disintegrate into metal knives that shredded body armor, giving the explosive brains access to zombie flesh.

Morphia smiled as a chopper's left 'forearm' detached from it in a gore-shower. She winced a moment later when its huge blade crashed onto a group of her soldiers, slicing all four of them in halves.

Mad at her carelessness, she ramped up the brain-cannon's inclination till it pointed directly into the chopper's cockpit. Time to end this chopper for good.

She now noticed the zombie in the helicopter aiming a brainshit mortar at her.

Shee-it! Flattening herself back in her seat, Morphia swivelled the gun sideways so the brainshit shell streaked between her and the firing mechanism. It demolished the wall of the hut behind her.

*That was too fucking damn close*, she thought, spinning the gun back around immediately and letting the chopper have it.

Its right fore-cleaver was already descending towards her when the shells exploded in the cockpit. She smirked at the mess of zombie gore that blew out through the helicopter's windows. The chopper began spiralling to a crash landing.

She realized it was falling at her.

She leapt out of the brain-cannon and ran like mad, ducking behind a hut as the chopper exploded, spraying biomechanical fragments everywhere.

All around her, the necros command raft was a flaming mingling of human and zombie flesh and helicopter remains.

Morphia grimaced, but in some satisfaction. Few of the zombie helicopters had survived their misguided assault on her territory. Her soldiers had given a kickass account of themselves. The fucking vegans would rethink greatly before attempting to attack a necros death raft again.

Then she spotted the group of three choppers, dangling nets full of necros captives, which had abandoned the fray and were fleeing back to DEZA lands.

*Oh no, you fucking don't,* Morphia thought. She ran through the carnage, pulling soldiers away from tending to the wounded wherever they could be spared.

She ensured a good portion of those she selected were 'augs'--necros with functional body augmentations cobbled together from salvaged zombie technology.

In particular, she looked for augs with hook-hands.

Once she'd gotten three 'hookies' with grappling hooks in place of fingers, she pointed to the escaping vegan craft.

"Get the hoverbikes out!" she screamed at them. "No way are those pieces of undead shit taking our kin back to plant potatoes in!"

#

The many explosions around him ensured Able Kane regained his wits quickly. He dashed through the surface-to-air/air-to-surface bombardment toward his hut. His mind was on retrieving his research and getting away with it alive.

The hut was still standing when he reached it. He ran inside and discovered that both the bedroom and lab were partly demolished.

Able groaned. He began rooting desperately through the destruction for his research papers. He found some, but the flesh-brick rubble lay too thick in places for him to get everything. Also, the explosions all around him were a constant reminder that he was here on borrowed time and had a limited window of opportunity to escape.

He didn't doubt Priest would shortly have men after him again.

He stopped collecting his papers, and opened the secret trapdoor in the floor concealing the results of his research. He secured the bottle of pink fluid inside his shirt and left the laboratory.

He now entered his bedroom to collect a few personal effects, throwing them into a small zombie-leather bag.

His xombina concubine lay in bed where he'd left her. Sighting him, she writhed sinuously as a snake. Able was uncertain if it was love or hatred etched on her face.

"Masterrrrr!"

Her legs were spread like bird wings in flight. Able stared at her open vagina with mingled twinges of desire and conscience. He mentally throttled his threatening erection.

Zombie cunt. The holy pus-lined slit granting entrance into the tunnel of undeath pleasance.

Remembering the pleasures her cunt had given him, Able felt it would be wrong to let the zombie girl get blown to bits.

He rolled her off the bed, then rolled her out of sight beneath it. He then pushed Morphia's dresser under the bed also, wedging it so she'd be unable to get out unaided.

"Don't come out and you'll be fine," he told her. Like one petting a dog, he ran a fond finger through her head-tree's leaves.

She would be. Like Neck in the holy hut.

An explosion outside rekindled Able's sense of urgency. He hurriedly collected his things: A brainshit-gun and box of shells, a knife, a gold chain and old gold coins; plus his copy of the Book of Undeath.

His taking this last object surprised him. He'd been much more affected by meeting God than he'd imagined.

"Massterrrr!"

*Shit,* Able thought, *what the hell now?* Surely she wasn't thinking of coming along with him?

"Massstteerrr!"

He knelt and peered underneath the bed into his concubine's huge white eyes.

"Yes?"

"You running away?"

Not bothering to wonder how she'd figured that out, he nodded.

She smiled dully. "I knew. You're a good person, Massstteerrr, you protect me. I will protect you too. Head for Avala. There is safety there."

With that, she rolled back into safety out of sight.

Able got back to his feet. She'd reminded him of something. He grabbed his jar of condom-worms. No telling where one might meet Miss Right-time. Or what species she'd be.

Safe sex kept one safe for more safe sex.

One last thing. He packed some food: Zombie sausages, eye-and-testis meatballs, strips of muscle jerky. And canteens of water.

Satisfied he'd gotten all he needed, he rushed out of the hut to find a bike.

Then he turned around and rushed back inside.

Damn his fucking conscience. He'd feel like shit forever more if he didn't take his damn xombina with him. He suspected Morphia would make her into vegan-jerky once she got back.

He'd take her with him, ditch her somewhere safe.

Able shook his head as he re-entered the bedroom. *Pussy is a disgustingly powerful thing,* he thought, *even stinky undead pussy.*

*The trouble a man's penis will get him into.*

He pulled away the dresser and looked under the bed again.

"Hey, come out here!" he called.

He was struck by the oddity that despite having fucked this xombina twice, he still didn't know her name. He hadn't even cared if she'd had one. He still didn't care. She still was less than shit, but still...

It was just awkward referring to her as 'hey' and 'you.'

Her face appeared. Her expression was one of slow-mo confusion.

"Massstttteerrr?"

"I can't leave you behind," Able said. "You're coming with me. We'll search for Avala together."

She smiled and rolled out to him.

Able got the key from the dresser and undid the chain on her neck.

They exited into the smoke and destruction outside.

Unnoticed by anyone, they made their way around smoking corpses and wrecked huts, around broken brain-cannons and helicopter fragments, to the nearest bike hut. With several of its stabilizers damaged, the death raft shuddered beneath them like a dying animal.

The zombie girl staggered against Able, her hair-tree against his cheek. Her stink of lemon chased away that of burning meat. She gripped him like he was salvation.

They ducked down behind a cleaver, peering around it to survey the bike hut from its rear.

Able studied his reflection in the gore-streaked metal. He looked haggard, totally unlike how he'd felt on waking. Then he'd felt sexed-out wonderful.

He momentarily cursed Priest.

He was unable to curse Neck... God, however.

His companion was touching the huge body-fingers of the hand gripping the weapon in wonder.

Able was also awed by the cleaver's size, but more so by the zombie technology that permitted its existence and operation. The metal blade was a tapering rectangular-square thrice his height in length and exactly his height in width. Its handle was as large as him and twice as thick.

And the real horrible genius of the vegans: Their use of their own flesh in their technology. Able feared the zombies for their lack of ethical reservations where science was concerned.

Each finger of the huge hand gripping the cleaver was a zombie body--headless, with arms, hands and feet removed, and both legs fused together. The knee was reversed to form a three-jointed digit. Four body-fingers and the short thumb (a 'finger' lacking the lower leg 'joint'). The palm of zombie torsos, and the arm of more full zombie bodies, all bolted together... Able had no idea how the vegan scientists got the raw material for their masterpieces--if they used those of their number too damaged to repair in their biomech constructs, or their criminals, or volunteers, or... just anyone who took their fancy or pissed them off.

Though he couldn't see the front, the approach to the hut seemed all-clear. Able pulled the zombie girl up, and then ducked again immediately.

He'd glimpsed a whirling reflection in the cleaver blade. The throwing knife soared over his head and pinged off the gleaming metal. It dropped into the mud. He stared at the weapon, recognizing the holy runes of undeath inscribed in its handle.

Shit! Priest had discovered he was gone. He looked up at his attackers: Two priests-- holy-assassins--with merciless eyes, and sadistic thin-lipped smiles.

"You are sentenced to death for heresy, Able Kane."

Able stole a glance at his companion. Double-shit! The second holy-assassin's knife had hit her in the left eye.

He watched in disbelief, while, struggling to pull the blade out, she over-balanced and toppled over.

*Noooo!* She fell in slow-motion, straight onto a patch of smeared brains.

Able turned away from the concert of soft explosions signalling her becoming chunks of zombie. Her head rolled over and bumped softly against his foot.

"Massteerrr!"

Able couldn't look at it. He cursed his penis for not letting him leave her safe below the bed.

Instead, he faced the approaching priests. Both walked slowly, with calm assurance of their kill, knowing their prey was no fighter.

"I'm no heretic, I believe in God the undead, She the glorious incarnation of Necro who walks amongst us."

"We have testimony of witnesses, Kane. For siding with the fallen angel Hereticos, Priest has ordered you to be both executed and incorporated into God's meat bed."

Shit, not the meat bed. Still there were worse fates for a necros than becoming divine food. He jerked the gun from his bag and aimed it at the priests.

"Her divinity can eat you instead."

Their smiles faltered.

He shot the assassin on the left in the face. To a muffled brainshit explosion, the man went down in a spray of brains. Half his head blown away, he twitched on the ground, pumping out blood.

Able had never killed a human before. He froze at the sight of the corpse he'd made, giving the second assassin time to close in on him and knock the gun from his hand.

The priest leaned in close to Able, his face contorted with rage.

"I'll make you pay for this you god-damned murderer."

He sank his fingers into Able's throat and squeezed.

Then he yelped and let go.

Able looked down. His xombina's severed head's teeth were clamped around the priest's ankle, savaging it. Blood streamed over her lips and over the man's foot.

Able needed no further encouragement. He quickly retrieved his gun from the floor and shot the priest, busy fighting to free his foot, twice in the back. He bent and picked up his concubine's head and ran for the bike hut.

Behind him, slow as a zombie, the dying priest slowly crumbled to the dust.

#

Able was about to enter the bike hut when Morphia zoomed out of it. He ducked back out of sight, watched eleven more bikes form a convoy after her, six with pillion women riders bearing brain-bazookas. Three of the riders were grapple-hands, with metal brainshit canisters on their backs.

The bikes were going full speed--two hundred miles an hour--speed guaranteed to more than double their brainshit consumption.

Able wondered at their waste of fuel till he spotted their helicopter quarry in the distance, tell-tale nets dangling from their undercarriages bulging with human cargo.

*Go girl go!* he thought angrily after the streaming bikes. *Get those fucks!* How dare vegans abduct necros.

Urgency reasserted itself on him. After a quick check to ensure all the other necros soldiers in sight were assisting the wounded, he entered the hut.

There were two hoverbikes left, both with full tanks. He chose one, activated its drive, loaded his belongings and his xombina's head into its storage compartment, and zoomed out of the hut.

He tracked Morphia's unit till he was off the death-raft, then swerved right, and streaked out across the worlderness.

No one saw him go.

# Chapter 8

Morphia's unit caught up with the choppers thirty miles from the burning raft. She gave the signal to slow down.

The necros formed into three four-bike teams, splitting off to engage the choppers four-on-one.

The attack plan was simple: Knock out each helicopter's control brain. With that gone, the choppers were worse than useless.

Because of the weight of their cleaver arms, choppers were low-altitude aircraft. Even unequipped with metal blades, they never flew higher than twenty feet. Laden with captives as now, they were restricted to fifteen.

Their burdens also meant a restriction to the degree of free motion their cleaver hands had. Situated behind the nets, the rear hands were useless. And their attackers would strike from behind.

DEZA lands were still a hundred miles distant. There was no way the zombies were reaching their home territory without winning this fight.

The zombies brought the fight. Zombie soldiers leaned out of the choppers and fired on the pursuing necros.

The necros responded in kind. Those with pillion-riding rocket-women rode out wide and harried the choppers with brain rockets. They fired wide of the cockpits. It would be pointless to kill the pilots--a crash would harm the captives also.

The rest of the necros steered with one hand and shot with the other to maintain the deceit.

Unaware of the ruse, the zombies ducked back into their craft to avoid splattering brains. Morphia smiled grimly. *Fucking veggies.*

She gave the rocket-women the thumbs up, then waved to the augs.

"Okay!" she yelled. "Go, go, go!"

While the others kept formation to the sides and rear of the choppers, the bikes with the augs zoomed beneath the nets to the loud encouragement of the captives.

The 'hookies' shot out their grapple-hands from their wrists. Thin metal cables unreeled from their arms behind the grapples.

With unerring precision, the grapples buried themselves in the chopper fuselage.

Once securely attached to the choppers, the hookies winched themselves up via geared engines in their shoulders, climbing up the helicopters' sides like mountaineers.

In moments all three augs were positioned on top of the helicopters, between their front and rear propellers.

In exact places, they broke through the choppers' shells. Then each unslung their brainshit bombs from their backs, activated them, and dropped them through the holes they'd made.

It was a textbook perfect military operation.

There was a chorus of muted explosions as the brainshit bombs took out each helicopter's guidance system--the human brains running them. Each chopper's front propeller instantly slowed and stopped spinning, forcing it to dip forward.

With too much weight for the rear propeller alone to support, the vehicles fell slowly to the ground, finally coming to rest 'standing' on their cleaver blades, looking like metal hounds, their rear propeller 'tails' whirling behind them in valiant but futile efforts to raise them aloft again.

Morphia laughed as she steered her hoverbike in close to the grounded choppers. The zombies peered out of the cockpits with fearful faces. They knew what to expect.

She licked her lips in anticipation. She was really going to enjoy butchering these shits. Too bad Able wouldn't be around to process them into food.

She realized she'd remembered Able Kane for the first time since they'd separated. She hoped the shithead hadn't got himself caught again.

Or exposed how she'd helped him get away if he had.

# Chapter 9

Ten miles out from Death Raft 4, Able encountered four death rafts floating towards him. They'd seen the smoke billowing from the capital raft and were coming to render help.

Able skirted the oncoming hovervillages. He'd no desire to be caught in a lie and returned home.

#

He rode for hours over miles and miles of unvarying sun-bleached terrain that made him feel he was simply hovering over the same spot. The only indication he had that he was moving at all was when he passed a lone cactus or sun-bleached skeleton.

Fifty miles, seventy-five, a hundred, two hundred, three-fifty, five hundred. The hoverbike's fuel gauge indicated half-full, then a third-full.

He needed to reach it soon.

Six-fifty. Seven hundred miles.

Then he saw the ruins of Texas and smiled. He was safe.

He slowed the bike and glided into the ancient town.

#

Just inside the sanctuary of the ruins, Able passed two leafy shrubs. He forgot them once they were behind him.

The shrubs didn't forget him, however. Or even let him out of their sight.

"Shsshhh, don't!" 219 whispered, when Soil attempted to hail Able Kane. She waited till he was a good distance away before explaining.

"He's a necros. He'll kill us."

Soil looked at her in surprise. "Why? He's human, like us. *And without leaves.*" This single fact made her want to leap on the strange man, and hug him as the expected fulfilment of her dreams.

"He's *extremely* dangerous. Necros hate zombies; but they hate humancows like us even worse than they hate zombies."

Soil stared at her. Once again she cursed her amnesia. 219 was clearly telling the truth--it angered her that she couldn't remember who the necros were.

Both womancows proceeded to follow Able Kane into Texas, ensuring they kept well out of sight and out of his way.

# Chapter 10

Morphia returned home to Death Raft 4 to a heroine's welcome.

The four death rafts Able Kane had passed while fleeing had now docked around the necros head raft, and the new arrivals were rendering aid and assistance to the wounded.

One of the newly arrived rafts instantly set out to retrieve the freed necros, who'd been left behind with the choppers to strip them of their technology. Their cleaver-wielding arms and hands would be in food processing vats before evening, along with the remains of the zombie attackers.

(To provide sufficient menstrual blood for purification of the anticipated meat overflow, those women from the assisting rafts who were on their periods formed lines outside the surviving food-processing huts to hand in their soaked tampon rats.

Women experiencing particularly heavy flows could sit on padded chairs beside the meat tanks, letting their menses run directly onto the meat via funnels built into the chairs.)

Death Raft 4 was damaged, but not crippled. Its repairs would take a while, but ironically, the technology removed from the many vegan choppers downed on it, and the three currently being dismantled out in the worlderness, would ensure its reborn form would be more imposing and powerful than its original incarnation.

## *Night the Before*

Later that night, Morphia was summoned into the holy hut for an audience with Priest and Neck.

Rather than in their living room, however, husband and wife received her in their bedroom. She sat on the meat bed between them, the smell of rotting humans in her nostrils, feeling the day's stress and adventure lift off her.

"You did well," Priest said, stroking her hair. "Able Kane escaped, however. He killed two priests and got away."

She feigned ignorance. "Able?" She disliked Priest's being intimate with her in God's presence.

"Yes," Neck said smiling at her. "He was sighted by our sister rafts as they approached. They thought he was on an urgent mission and didn't stop him." She laid a bony arm on Morphia's thigh and stroked it.

Morphia realized husband and wife wanted to fuck her together. This was something she hadn't expected. Herself and Priest had each seduced the other, but... she realized she'd naively erased Neck out of the equation in her fantasy of becoming necros queen.

She smiled at Neck, bent and kissed Priest. Screw it, power was power, no matter how convoluted the alleys one trod to acquire it, or associations one made to get it. Assistant queen would do just as well.

Neck laughed. Morphia and Priest laughed in response. The trio fell back into the bed of corpses and maggots and fucked vigorously.

#

Morphia was enjoying her first three-way sex scene.

She lay moaning on Neck, suckling God's breasts while she fucked her cunt. Priest filled her from behind with his short fat cock. It hurt, but pleasantly.

Then they switched positions. Priest lay beneath her, Neck above. Morphia braced herself to accept Neck's cock in her slackened and slickened anus, but disappointingly, it didn't come.

She felt empty. She moaned, "My god, my God; fill me with yourself."

She heard the sucking sound of something being pulled out of the bed meat.

She looked back saw Neck was holding a huge thighbone, greasing it with gore and maggots.

Next she felt it hard between her ass cheeks and pushing into her anus.

"No lord!" she moaned. "My Lord of Fuck!" Beneath her, Priest continued to pump her pussy and knead her breasts.

"No lord!" she screamed as the huge orb of the femur's upper ball forced its way past her sphincter, widening her to ripping point. It was larger than a penis and bent at an angle. God, God, God, God, God.

Despite calling on all her warrior experience of coping with pain, she whimpered like a scared sand rat; calling for help: "Oh Godddddd, help me!!!" Fittingly.

Ignoring her, Neck forced the thighbone deep inside Morphia's body. She smiled at the ass-blood trickling down its white length, navigating its way between still-attached meat.

Morphia's muted screams agitated the xombinas chained to the wall. They stared restively at the screwing trio. Two finger-fucked their rotted cunts.

Her noises bored Priest. He silenced her by twisting their bodies sideway and forcing her head into the gore. He didn't let her up for air till her mouth was full of maggots.

God smiled beatifically at Morphia's buttocks as she thigh-boned her.

## Morning the after

Morphia woke up with the thighbone still stuck up her ass. She snorted and spat, clearing her nostrils and throat of maggots.

Beside her, Priest and God snored loudly.

She lay quietly between them in the gore-bed and thought.

The sex had been mind-blowing, but there were more important things to consider: Her future, for one.

Morphia was no fool. She knew Neck would only tolerate her as long as Priest wanted her.

She would *make* Priest *want* her.

She was a good-looking woman, he a very ugly man--there was no contest.

She reached down and plucked the bone's ball and socket joint from her anus, feeling the pop of its coming free and the rush of rotten water and maggots entering her rectum in its place.

Her ass hurt like hell, but it was a divine pain and a blessed one, one to be savored for bringing her closer to holiness and power.

# Chapter 11

Breakfast was marred by the discovery of Able Kane's left-behind research papers.

With Able gone, his assistant Beni, a tall dour man who'd long resented living in his shadow, had wasted no time proving his efficiency. Part of this had necessitated a dawn trip to Able and Morphia's destroyed hut to search its rubble for a number of papers Able had taken home to work on.

Beni had been ecstatic; then much less so when he'd discovered his runaway boss's left-behind research papers.

Disbelieving Able's madness, he'd at once brought them to Priest.

"Have a seat and some zombie sausages," Morphia invited while Priest perused the documents before him.

"Thank you, Madam," Beni returned politely. He sat and ate what she dished out for him. He concealed his amusement at finding her here, clearly for the long haul, so soon after Able's heresy had been discovered. *Women.* Maybe she'd turned him in even.

He ensured, however, he was politely deferent to Morphia. *She was dangerous.*

If she *had* betrayed Able, she'd done him the favor he'd needed for ages. If she *hadn't,* she might resent him stepping into her lover's shoes.

She was clearly with Priest to ensure that her own position as security chief remained secure. *Women.* Unfortunately disgust would prove a counterproductive emotion here.

He smiled insincerely at Morphia. "These sausages are delicious, madam."

Her replying smile was equally insincere. She'd never liked or trusted Beni, but he had power now, and she needed all the political allies she could get.

The storm Beni had been awaiting broke just as he finished his last bite of zombie. Priest dropped the papers and gaped at him. The head necros looked about to have a heart attack.

"He... he... Is it possible?"

Beni nodded deferentially. "Yes lord, it is."

"He can actually do this thing, make this liquid?"

"Yes Lord Priest. Kane is a genius, a total misfit as a human. He should have been born a zombie." The words rankled to say, but Beni was honest. He admitted to himself Able's brilliance was the primary reason he'd resented working under him--it meant there was no chance of kicking him out.

Morphia had picked up the papers and was looking through them.

"Let me get this straight," Priest said. "Able Kane is able to alter human flesh, make it unsuitable for growing blood potatoes?"

"Yes my lord." Beni was growing uncomfortable. He'd expected Priest to be displeased, but the man looked like he'd regurgitate his breakfast from horror. "He records success, though other than several preserved human hands in his personal lab, I found no evidence. He must have taken the formula with him."

Priest turned to Morphia, his gaze black. "You knew nothing of this?"

Morphia put down the papers. Her white face was more skeletal than normal. She shook her head. "No." It worried her how unconvinced Priest looked. She wasn't far now from suspicion that she'd helped Able escape.

"She didn't know, Lord Priest," Beni said. It made sense to have her as an ally. "Able hid everything in a hole he'd hollowed out of the floor of their hut. He apparently also only worked when Madam Morphia was out on business."

Priest nodded. "The bastard's that smart, eh?"

Beni nodded.

Morphia dared speak. "I don't understand. What harm does Able curing the humancows do? It only accelerates the coming of the true kingdom of Necro, when zombie will have to eat man, and the food cycle will be perfect, does it not?"

Beni nodded also.

Priest smiled sadly. "In any other case, yes. But in this case, no. When Able Kane spoke yesterday, accusing the divine Neck of lying, he was specific that he would save humankind, would be their messiah."

He nodded at both shocked faces. "You don't have to take my word for it--there are witnesses."

Neither spoke, so he went on, his voice pained. "Able Kane intends to set up his own kingdom here on Earth. Unlike we necros who believe in eating zombie and being eaten by them, Able's intention is to starve zombies out of existence completely." His voice fell to a whisper. "If he saves the humancows, what is to stop him overrunning Neo La, the DEZA stronghold itself?"

"No one is that mad!" Beni gasped, his ears burning from the horrible idea. "If he kills the zombies, he destroys the necros way of life also! He wouldn't!"

"He *would*," Morphia said softly. "You've no idea what Able is like once he gets an idea in his head."

She bowed to Priest. "Able Kane will do inestimable damage if he is permitted to apply this cure of his. I will travel and find him and kill him before he has the chance to begin."

Priest smiled sadly at her. "I hope you succeed my dear, or else the end is upon us and the entire re-creation."

# Chapter 12

Morphia left Death Raft 4 at noon. She rode alone, both from a feeling of responsibility for the mess at hand, and from the knowledge that any companions would slow her down.

In addition to her guns, she was armed with a pair of long bone swords sculpted from the thighbones of a zombie giant. She'd run out of ammo sooner or later. Her zombie swords, however, would never lose their thirst for blood.

Or their edge. With the right treatments, zombie bone could be worked sharper than steel. And harder too.

Morphia rode a specially upgraded hoverbike, an 'extreme situations' zombie model. In addition to carrying over a month's store of food and water, it was equipped with four auxiliary brainshit tanks. She could ride for thousands of miles.

She doubted, however, that she'd need to ride that far. In this instance, seven hundred miles should be quite far enough.

She was certain Able had fled to Texas. He always liked that place. He had no need to go farther than there, seeing as no one else other than Morphia would know to look for him there.

Her ass burnt from last night's sex as she rode. The pain spurred her on. *Able, you shit,* she thought, *I'm coming to kill you before you kill all of us!*

Part Three:
In Blood (Potatoes) We Trust

# Chapter 1

Warden Painfield surveyed the corpses in shocked disgust.

It was inconceivable that humancows could escape from *her* farm.

She looked angrily at Brainchild, the vegfarm security chief.

"So much for psychological prison walls then. Do we know who's gone?"

Brainchild shook his head. He was a short zombie with a plastic patch covering part of his face where the skin had completely rotted away.

"No, Warden. We felt it best not to alert our other cows to the fact that two of their number got out alive. Several chopper search patrols are out looking for them now. It's most likely they'll find them and bring them back."

Painfield considered a moment. This was true; it was unwise planting escape ideas in minds whose parent bodies had unwanted potatoes planted in them.

If the search patrols found the fugitives, she'd have them both harvested instantly. Their crop could waste for all she cared. Their brains and excrement wouldn't.

She was struck by a thought. "Ask the men. They might have noticed their IDs."

Brainchild departed to question the guards who'd witnessed the escape.

Painfield watched them discuss with dark thoughts. Something was wrong here. She could sense it.

Vegan military psychologists asserted that a humancow's emotional conditioning was an unseen chain it could never break free of, an invisible cell the bars of which it could never get through. They could *think* of fleeing. Indeed, it was *desirable* that they dream of escaping the farm--hope kept their minds and bodies healthy and ensured healthy potato crops. But they'd *never* have the initiative to take steps towards making the dream come true.

An unattainable dream was all escape ever would be to a humancow.

And that was all it had ever been. In all Painfield's time as warden, no vegfarm humancow had ever dared raise a violent hand against a zombie. Neither had she ever heard of such from sister vegfarms.

So what had gone wrong now?

Brainchild returned.

"The men say one of the womancows was busy stealing a hoverbike--they didn't see her ID number. But the other one, who threatened them with a catapult of brains, her ID was Soil-15f."

*Soil-15f. Dr. October's pet project.*

She was suddenly certain the searchers would return empty-handed. Just as she was certain it was 15f's numbersake 15m who'd stolen the multikey.

Brainchild confirmed as much. "They say the cows had a multikey."

Brainchild noticed Painfield's pained expression.

"Warden... warden, are you okay?

Painfield caught herself. "I'm fine," she lied. "It's just your mention of brains just now." There was no point letting Brainchild know how much trouble hovered on all their horizons.

"Brainchild."

He stood smartly to attention. "Yes, Warden."

"Clean up the mess," she said curtly. "And once it's dawn, have a roll call and find out who the second escapee was."

She went to place a call to Dr. October.

# Chapter 2

This time Painfield wasn't pleased at all having the Doctor's balls in her grip.

Not minding the time, the doctor had flown over immediately once she'd explained the problem on the phone.

It was now four in the morning. The pair of them sat facing each other in her office.

The search teams had returned empty-handed an hour ago. There was no sign of the missing womancows.

"Doc, I think it's time you tell the big secret," she said softly. "Why are your two 15ses so important?"

She almost felt sorry for Dr. October. He was doing his best to conceal his agitation, and only barely succeeding. *Screw him,* she thought. If blame was going to be shared out, this was more his fault than hers. If he'd explained, she'd have taken firmer precautions.

And she *still* didn't know what the fuss was.

"Yes, it's time," the doctor agreed. "I'd have told you next week anyway, when we harvested them. Do you still have the other one in custody? The male 15?"

"Yes."

The doctor sighed his relief. "You were right to hold onto him; else they'd have escaped together. They're a breeding pair."

He waited for the implications of his statement to sink in, then laughed bitterly. "Sixteen years of research and it runs away five days to being harvested."

Painfield looked at him perplexed. She was disappointed by the anticlimax of his big revelation. "*That's* your big secret? That they can have children together? Doc, the ordinary humans we catch and make into meatfields everyday can do that."

Dr. October got wearily to his feet. "Let's go visit your captive, warden."

\#

After discovering Soil's unprecedented escape, Painfield had taken no chances on 15m following suit. Despite realizing she was simply being paranoid, she'd doubly secured the mancow.

15m lay on a table, doped out of his mind. His arms and legs were each secured by metal chains that vanished out of sight in the foliage around his ankles and wrists.

Dr. October had been silent during the walk between office and cell. He resumed speaking only when the cell door shut behind them, leaving them alone.

"We're running out of *ordinary* humans, warden," he said. "Running the number of vegfarms we do--six thousand and fifty-three at my last asking--we're down to our last five percent of mankind to use as farmland. Those humans still living wild in the worlderness will be gone in two years flat, *one* if the DEZA council keeps refusing to reduce the number of lavish parties they throw."

His words shocked Painfield. She'd never thought zombiehood could run out of human cattle. She stared at 15m. *But what use...?*

Dr. October saw he had her full attention. "You know what happens don't you, once we vegans no longer have blood potatoes?"

Painfield grimaced. "We degenerate back into the shambling horrors of ancient human movies." She was horrified. The future would be the past, and so soon. "This runaway womancow of yours... how?"

The doctor tapped 15m's chest, rifled his leaves with a finger. "You were right in your earlier observation." It's not just breeding that makes Soil 15f and her numbersake special. For another thing they're both only two years and six months old."

He smiled at Painfield's surprised expression, gestured at 15m with a smile. "Yes, I lied--they weren't transfers from a farm nursery. Both were grown in my laboratory. We gave them false memories so they think they're older.

"The primary problem with using humans as farmland is the time it takes them to grow to adulthood. Child flesh doesn't breed good food for us."

"So you're saying..." Her brow furrowed. "Two and half years is an improvement, and their children too?"

He nodded. "They'll have lots of them. Breed like the proverbial swine. No... like insects, like bees." He parted 15m's groin vines, exposing his huge balls. "That's why this bull's testicles are so big."

He began walking around Painfield while speaking. She found this disorienting, so she went and leaned against a wall so she could view the whole cell at once, pacing scientist inclusive.

"There's another difference between 15f and 15m and the normal humancow. They're reusable."

"*What?*"

"Yes. I did say reusable. Both 15f and 15m have only been here two years, but unknown to them both, their blood potatoes will be ripe by next week. We don't need to kill them before harvesting. General anesthetic will do. After that we simply re-cultivate them again--stick new seeds in their existing muscle tunnels--ad infinitum."

"Two years to grow potatoes? Over and over again?"

"Much less even than that. Those were our first generation breed. My research team has developed a new potato strain that matures in three months, like ancient potatoes did. The catch is--they'll only grow in the flesh of these new genetic 15ses."

The doctor sighed painfully. "There's one more thing. 15f and 15m are the only two of their kind we bioengineered successfully. There are no others. The pair of them *are* the food revolution."

He stopped pacing, walked over to 15m. After a moment staring at the face of the doped mancow, he bent over his chest and twined his fingers around a vine.

He yanked the blood potato out of 15m's body.

It came free in a spray of blood, strips of muscle and flesh dangling from it. 15m's eyes remained closed, his breathing remained even.

"I haven't really harmed him," Dr. October said, absentmindedly peeling the shreds of human skin off the tuber. The blood potato wiggled its odd unlife dance of pseudo-pain, its vegetable face contorting like it could hear them. "This new breed of human is super-tough. Indeed if they'd evolved as a species on their own they'd rule the earth, even we zombies."

Dangling the wiggling potato between them like a pennant, he stared directly into Painfield's bulbous eyes.

"I'm telling you this, warden," he concluded grimly, "so you'll fully understand the gravity of the situation we're in. We need to get that womancow back, whatever the cost. And unharmed. The future of zombiehood depends on her."

He stuffed the blood potato back into its hole in 15m's chest.

"I understand," Painfield said in a ghost's voice. "We don't catch her, and we're back in the zombie stone age again."

The thought, and its imminence, horrified her.

# Chapter 3

## *Death and the King's Zombinator*

There was a 666m, but he was nothing like humancow legend represented him.

666 was a seven-foot-tall zombie. As muscled as the fabled minotaur. He was nude, but his body was inlaid with so much metal and plastic he appeared clothed.

His myriad implants were body armor and weaponry.

666 was zombiehood's top bounty hunter.

He tracked and returned vegan criminals. He also tracked and assassinated any humans in the worlderness who threatened to upset the DEZA-dominated status quo.

666 and other augs like him were called 'zombinators.'

He sat now in Painfield's office, his face impassive, beside a woman.

Death wasn't a zombie, though her skin had the same unhealthy undead pallor as theirs. She *was* Death; a version of mankind's final termination specially adapted by Necro for life in his re-creation.

Death had an incredibly voluptuous female body and a totally horrible face. Her eyes bulged like a zombie's. Her nose was a penis-long tube.

Worst of all was her mouth. It was an actual wound in her jaw. It looked like someone had attacked her face with a meat cleaver--a horrible lipless unhealed wound that bubbled blood like saliva.

Chunks of fractured bone jutted irregularly through the meat of the opening-- Death's teeth. Her tongue was a little muscle flapping amidst the gore.

She had no ears. Their lack was concealed by her hair--long and black and glossy and hanging halfway down her back.

Death wore a black catsuit.

666 and Death had partnered together only recently, discovering they shared an interest in the affliction of pain on others. They were also lovers, 666's augmentations including a 'fucktioning' biometal penis.

Painfield nodded to her guests.

She was close to being overwhelmed by the sheer scale of the responsibility now placed on her shoulders.

The greatest breakthrough in zombie history and half of it had run off, was out there somewhere, Necro knew where.

She silently cursed Dr. October and his damn secrecy. She understood he'd done it so as not to raise false hopes, but there was such a thing as taking 'need to know' too far.

One word about 15f's importance and she'd have kept the womancow under lock and key like her boyfriend. And why the hell had they brought her to a farm anyway? Why not just keep the bitch safe in his lab, or give the pair their own private farm? Shit.

"You understand that everything we've discussed is of course totally confidential?" she asked.

666 nodded. "Your womancow will be recaptured, warden. Don't worry. She will be returned silently to your clutches."

Death spoke in her cold voice. "Once we determine where she is, the rest will be easy."

Painfield disliked Death. It wasn't just jealousy over the fact that she wasn't decaying. The goddess's horrid face was something she could do without seeing.

But she needed them--the pair of them were *super*-effective at retrievals.

More important, they were super-discreet. Whichever way this mess turned out, she and Dr. October could count on their silence.

She nodded. "Perfect."

The pair rose and left.

Her bounty hunters gone, Warden Painfield walked to her office window and stared out over the farm she supervised.

Watching her herds of mancows and womancows walking towards the cafeteria for the morning's feed of past humancows, she couldn't shake the feeling that disaster was imminent.

Her thoughts were broken into by a knock on the door.

"Come in."

Death entered again, carrying a small cardboard box. She smiled at Painfield.

"We almost forgot. Dr. October asked us to give you this. He called it *protection*, a safeguard in case things don't work as planned."

Painfield frowned at the box. "He never said anything to me about this."

"It slipped his mind. He'll call you later."

She bowed. "I'll be leaving now."

Death left again.

When she'd shut the door behind her, Painfield shrugged and opened the cardboard box.

*What...?* It was packed full of brains.

She heard the click of its trigger mechanism activating.

The bomb exploded, splattering Painfield all over with brains.

Painfield exploded the next moment, splattering her office walls with chunks of herself.

## Chapter 4

666 and Death headed out over the worlderness in a small military helicopter.

They weren't alone. They were accompanied by a crew of six zombinators. Augmented 'aug' zombies like 666, but smaller. Three male, three female. And all totally remorseless and inexorable.

They were getting back that stupid 15f runaway womancow meatfield no matter what.

# Part Four:
# Connections and Disconnections

# Chapter 1

Soil and 219 watched Able Kane for a whole day before attempting to talk to him.

"He doesn't look too dangerous," Soil said. "He's done nothing since arriving here but sit and look miserable and stare at that tree."

Her body ached like mad now. The one thing she and 219 had overlooked during their planning was medication. Without the numbing zombie drugs, she felt she was swimming through an ocean of pain with every step.

Her muscles hurt like she'd gladly cut them off to be rid of them. She could practically feel the blood potatoes leeching her life's blood away.

From the look on 219's fat face, she felt just as bad.

"Damn we should have tried to steal painkillers," she growled. "I feel like shit!"

She pulled their last two chunks of meat out of her cuntbag and grimaced. "We're out of food." She looked over at the house where Able was holed up. "By tomorrow we'll have to consider eating him."

In principle, Soil agreed with her. No point starving with food available. Still: "I think we should talk to him," she said. "Maybe he'll share his food with us."

"He's eating zombie meat."

*"Huh?"*

"Yeah. He's *necros*. Zombies are their religion--they eat and fuck 'em. Live in houses built from them. Even wear 'em as clothes."

She laughed mockingly. "They expect zombies to return the favor, but the vegans aren't interested." Her expression turned thoughtful. "It's odd, him being here all alone though. They're normally very clannish."

"He's on the run like us," Soil said. "Only explanation which makes sense."

219 took a bite of meat, gave the second chunk to Soil. "Better for us then. No one will miss him when we eat him."

Soil stared sharply at the fat womancow. "Is food all you think about?"

"What's gotten into you? He isn't one of us. We kill and eat him to survive."

"I think we should team up with him." Soil wasn't deceiving herself that they would be safe in Texas very long. Best to get out of here. Maybe the necros man had an idea where they could head. Neither she nor 219 did.

"I've told you he's dangerous and can't be trusted. Besides, it's creepy the way he stares at that tree all the time."

Soil agreed with 219. Able Kane did appear mad. The tree he was growing seemed to be all he cared about, as though he'd travelled to Texas for that purpose.

"Okay, you wait here and watch," she said. "I'll talk to him." She picked up a large rock and handed it to 219. "If he attacks me, spill his brains with this. We'll have him for dinner."

She set off for Able's position.

#

The tree the womancows were referring to was the one which had initially been planted in Able's concubine's head.

By the time Able Kane arrived in Texas, his xombina's head had degenerated to a dead skull with a bonsai lemon tree planted in it-- the result of the holy-assassin's blood entering her mouth when she bit his ankle to save Able. Poisonous as meat to zombies, the blood had dissolved her flesh and mind away during the trip.

(Able felt shitty about the zombie girl dying before he'd even learnt her name. He'd fucked her, then saved her, then she'd saved him, then they'd fled [sort of] together, and now this.

Necro truly worked in mysterious ways.)

Since reaching the ruined city, the bonsai tree had been growing rapidly. By the time Able had been in Texas for two hours, it had outgrown and fractured its skull pot.

A true scientist, he'd been more intrigued than worried. He'd taken the tree out into the front yard of the house he was sheltering in and planted it.

He was glad for the puzzle it presented. It took his mind off his flight from his people and his proposed trip to Avala.

It occurred to Able that the tree might call attention to itself, and by extension, to him. But he doubted it would grow sufficiently large enough to do so.

How wrong he was.

The lemon tree grew fast. By his second day there, it was as tall as himself, and half as wide. It was also beginning to fruit lemons.

There was one thing about his tree, however, which Able didn't really understand. It had two side-by-side short tubes set four feet up from its base.

Each was red and looked like a length of small intestine. Each also had a notice pegged above it that read: 'Blow me.'

At first Able was *very* dubious about blowing into the tubes. But the tree stopped growing after they appeared, so it occurred to him that aerating the tubes was the next line of action.

He'd just decided to blow into the tubes and watch what happened, when Soil hailed him.

He turned and saw her, saw she was unarmed, and relaxed somewhat.

A womancow? And out here?

Soil saw his surprise and realized Able wasn't dangerous at all. "I escaped," she said, remembering just in time that she was supposed to be alone, in case he actually *was* dangerous. "I fled my farm."

Able nodded at the leaf-covered woman. "15f?" Her eyes, and the studied way she moved told him she was in pain.

She smiled a hint of rotten teeth. "Call me Soil."

"I'm Able Kane," he said. "My people are after me to kill me also--for breach of religious etiquette." He offered her his hand.

She took it, shook it. "We're friends then."

Able nodded. "Yes, friends."

She was someone to be with. She was, of course, shit for refusing to live by Necro's decrees. She was much less than his last turd for permitting herself to be caught and made into farmland, but just like his xombina, she was *someone*.

And... and...

A thrill of anticipation went through Able. Looking the leaf-covered woman over, he realized that here was someone on whom he could finally use his humancow cure.

He smiled reassuringly at her. "I'm about to blow into my tree, maybe you can help me."

Bemused, Soil followed him to the tree.

#

Soil and Able each took a tube and huffed and puffed.

Like a balloon, the lemon tree inflated. Like Jack's beanstalk, it grew and grew and grew.

"This wasn't a good idea, was it?" Soil said as the expanding girth of the tree pushed them backwards, growing up thick roots beneath their feet that lifted them off the ground.

"Looks like not," Able replied. They leapt down and ran for the house, the tree-trunk expanding rapidly behind them as they went, threatening to crush them into the building's walls. They made it through the door safely.

The lemon tree smashed through the wall of the house and stopped.

"I think it's stopped growing," Able Kane said.

"Uh huh," Soil agreed.

They walked back outside through another door for a look.

The lemon tree now appeared to reach to Haeven, where Necro resided.

"We've just set up a major marker as to our location," Soil said. "Best we get out of here immediately. I'll call my friend."

"Not yet," Able said, then: "Friend? I thought..."

"We weren't sure you were safe." She frowned. "Be careful with her--don't give her any excuse to attack you. She thinks you're food."

Able nodded. "Uh huh." He was glad he had his gun. "Okay, fetch her, I want to check this tree, see where it goes."

"Where it goes?"

He pointed to the bottom rungs of a ladder, just projecting beneath the tree's lowest leaves. "It certainly goes somewhere; maybe somewhere *interesting*."

Soil looked at the necros. Maybe he was insane after all. She raised her hands and waved at where 219 was hiding. She waited till 219 waved back, then turned back to Able.

"Where are you initially headed?"

She was in a lot of pain now, needed to lie down somewhere peaceful and rest. Her mind drifted back to the vegfarm cafeteria where there were loads and loads of roasted people to feed on. What was the point of fleeing--was there one?

The drugs, the drugs, she needed medicine.

Maybe being out here in the worlderness wasn't worth it. Maybe it was better to fulfill her womancow destiny, growing food for zombie almighty.

She shook her head clear. Fuck that. No way was she returning. And if this man became more trouble than he was worth, she'd eat his balls and his cock too, just like that nutcase 69f, and enjoy it.

"Avala," Able replied. "I was advised to go there for safety."

"Where is it?"

"I don't know."

"Didn't the person who advised you give you directions?"

Able winced. Though coming from this under-my-shit person, it was a valid question. "We were heading there together." He pointed up. "She became the tree."

"The tree?"

*"Seriously."*

"So you think Avala might be up there? In Haeven?"

"Avala's a myth," 219 said, joining them then. "I'd have expected a necros like you to know that."

They both turned to her. "My friend 219," Soil said, "tact isn't her strong point."

"No offense taken," Able said. He smiled at the womancow. "I'm a friend."

219 scowled. "Necros are never friends of cows."

"He's on the run like us," Soil said. "We're friends of circumstance."

#

They debated what to do.

"This damn tree's been seen everywhere around by now," 219 said. She and Soil were both eating some zombie sausage Able had given them.

"This is good," Soil said. "Better than human meat even."

"Man was created by Necro to eat zombie," Able said. "And vice versa." He looked from face to face. "Someone, or lots of someones will be arriving here very soon. I suggest we climb the tree."

"I agree," 219 said. "We're desperate to get away. It's unlikely anyone's *that* desperate to catch us."

"It's agreed then?" Able asked. "We climb the tree?"

Soil nodded.

"We climb the damn tree," 219 agreed.

# Chapter 2

The gigantic lemon tree *had* been noticed.

## 1

Fifty miles from Texas, Morphia parked her bike and stared up at the huge plant.

From this far out it was a slim vine linking Earth and Haeven. It definitely reached Haeven, she was certain of it.

She groaned. *Able Kane.* It had to be Able Kane.

## 2

A hundred miles east of Texas, Death and her helicopter-load of zombinators also noticed the black thread bisecting the sky.

"What's out there?" 666 asked.

"Texas," Death replied. "Old ruins, nothing there. Except now there is."

"Coincidence maybe."

"Or maybe not."

She swung the helicopter towards Texas.

# Chapter 3

Like a fire-escape, the lowest segment of ladder folded down so they could climb it.

After hiding their bikes, they ascended it. 219 first, Able last. In addition to packing food and water, Able had taken the time to remove his bike's brainshit tank.

"We might need explosives," he told both womancows.

For a while it was an uneventful climb. The tree went up and up and up, higher than any of them had ever been before.

They were saved from vertigo by the thick leaf shield, which prevented them from noticing how far away the ground was, except they intentionally parted the leaves for a peek.

Soil took one such peek and vowed never to take another.

Then they reached the first platform.

Invisible from the ground, it was twenty feet wide and made of branches placed over branches, like one would do if building a raft.

They collapsed in exhaustion.

"Thank Necro," Able said. "A rest is long over--"

"GRRRRR!"

The trio jumped up to face the creature emerging from around the tree trunk.

Seeing it, all three immediately got their weapons out. .

The creature was zombie, but of a sort none of them had ever seen before. Though it stood upright, it looked more like a beast than a man. It was six feet tall. Its legs were hinged like a dog's, with three joints. Its decaying skin was white and long-furred and covered with red spots. It had bloodshot eyes, triangular ears, a hairy projecting muzzle and huge fangs, and claws designed to shred flesh.

It approached them in a crouch, an unholy hunger in its eyes.

"A zombie werewolf or were-zombie," Able said, horrified. "One of the disgusting creatures of Hereticos locked behind in Hell when the cuntdoors to the netherworld were blocked by the zombies."

Able's religious crisis was deepening. Two days ago, he'd believed the creature standing beside him an old wives' tale, something he'd never dignify with belief, and now he was face to face with one.

Brain-loaded catapults in hand, both womancows inched to either side of the were-zombie, wary of its jaws and claws, but not cowed.

The creature paused its approach. It stared at the two womancows in some confusion. They smelled good to eat, but also looked and smelled like plants.

"Come on, bitch," 219 growled at it, catapult held at the ready. "We got brains for you, like grandma used to make--raw straight from the skull."

"Brains won't kill it," Able said. "Its werewolf aspect protects the zombie from harm."

"Then what?" 219 asked, not taking her eyes from the were-zombie's carmine orbs. No way was this piece-of-shit monstrosity having her for lunch after all the crap she'd been through.

She nodded at Able's gun. *"Shoot it then."*

He sighed. "Bullets won't kill it either, they'll just make it mad."

Beads of sweat had formed on his forehead and were running into his eyes. He was very scared--too scared to hide his fear because there were less-than-shit people present.

Both 'cows looked at him in equal fear.

The zombie-wolfman stepped closer to them, licking its chops, still perplexed by the immixed meat-vegetable smell both womancows gave off. Yellow rot-pus dripped from its right ear. The closer it got to them, the more aware they became of its rotting-meat smell.

"Then what the fuck will?" Soil whimpered.

"Nothing we've got close at hand. Shit, brainshit explosives will, but I've no time to set them up."

Soil gaped at him incredulously. "So what do we do?"

"We trick it over the edge."

The plan came too late, however.

The were-zombie made up its mind and attacked, leaping at Able Kane with salivating lips. *He* had no confusion of smells to him. He was just plain meat.

Able went down under the beast's charge. As he fell he fired.

The bullet pushed the were-zombie back three inches, and threw it off its aim to rip out his throat, but that was all. Slobbering saliva on him, it crashed down on Able onto the platform edge.

He had the briefest of glimpses of the worlderness, an eternity of breakneck falling down below, and of something totally unexpected--a helicopter hovering by the tree's lower reaches.

Then the were-zombie bit into his shoulder, and he went mad with pain and rage.

Able Kane had never thought of himself as particularly courageous, but he wasn't dying here and now. Not in some bullshit way like this.

The were-zombie's teeth were deep in his shoulder muscle. His zombie-plait jacket, however, resisted its attempts to rip the flesh of him.

Its stink of dog-corpse was thick in his nostrils.

Able never considered the irony of his being protected from a zombie-by-zombie clothing. Quickly, before the creature wizened up and attacked his throat again, he stiffened the fingers of his right hand and dug them hard into its right eye.

The were-zombie shrieked in pain, attempted to rear up. Able refused to let it go. He pulled down on it with his left arm. He dug his right-hand fingers still deeper into its skull till he was holding/squeezing its eye, then yanked it out of the were-zombie's head. Then while the two womancows watched in horrified admiration, he ate the eye, chewing it so the were-zombie could appreciate what he intended doing to it.

"Eat zombie!" he screamed like a supplicant in the Temple of Undeath.

The creature now fought to get away from Able. It had lost all thought of feeding. All it wanted was to flee back to the black depths of Hell it had emerged from.

It pushed violently against Able's chest and reared up, only to be instantly knocked back down and out cold, by Soil and 219, who between them wielded a huge fallen branch.

"Where'd you think your hairy ass is going eh, bitch?" 219 asked the bashed-in rear of the were-zombie's head as it crumbled down beside Able.

#

Before it could awaken, Able cut off the were-zombie's head.

"That takes care of that shit," he said, dropping it a short distance from the creature.

He pointed to the gently trembling body and handed Soil his knife. "Here's food. Stuff your cuntbags with as much as you like."

219 shook her head. "Zombie meat is poison to humans."

Able nodded. "Not this sort. The werewolf trace makes it edible, just like it prevents brains from killing it. That's what the scriptures teach."

He sighed at her still-unconvinced look. "I just ate its eye didn't I? And I'm still fine."

He gestured impatiently at the quivering body. "Hurry up, and let's go--there's a zombie helicopter down there that has to be looking for you two."

He left them looking scared and went to peer out between the leaves.

Soil and 219 got to work, skinning the were-zombie and slicing off its thigh, arm, and chest meat and stuffing it up into themselves for safekeeping.

Able took a break from his watching to throw them his bag. They stuffed it as full of meat as its other contents would allow.

The were-zombie's head recovered its senses while they worked. With its remaining eye it gaped in incomprehension at their progressive destruction of its body.

"We're done," Soil called finally. 219 was busy draping herself in tripe like she was a meat-rack.

Able moved away from the leaf covering. He liked the look of both cows now. Except for their covering of leaves and vines, both could be mistaken for necros.

Priest was wrong. If these two womancows had so easily adopted the 'eat zombie' truth there was no reason to think other humancows would be any different.

Humankind, heretics all, needed saving from themselves, and he, Able Kane was their unexpected and unprecedented messiah.

Basking in anticipation of his future glory, Able Kane kicked the were-zombie head off the platform.

He joined Soil and 219 and they resumed their ascent, all three still uncertain where they were headed.

#

Morphia swerved her hoverbike just in time.

The were-zombie head smashed into the dust-submerged road directly in front of her. It ricocheted twice off walls, then rolled to a halt.

She climbed off her bike and inspected it.

Morphia had never seen a were-zombie before. She, however, knew their description, as well as what the scriptures said about them-- the cursed zombies who were part-human, part-wolf.

This was clearly one such.

But who'd fucked it up so badly? These things were supposed to be super tough.

Able? That wimp?

She looked up at the monster tree dominating the middle of Texas. She was two hundred meters from it. Thrown from high enough up, this head could have come from there, which would mean the shithead was climbing. She laughed disparagingly. It was quintessential Able, to climb, to keep seeking answers to unasked questions. And where the fuck did he think he was headed? Haeven? He had inquiries for Necro too now?

For some reason this last thought bothered her greatly.

Her dumb ex was smart enough to screw up Haeven itself, given half the chance.

The undead head whimpered at her piteously. Its huge canines were all broken off now, and in crashing to earth it had bitten through its tongue, severing it almost in two.

Morphia felt sympathy for the creature-- it surely regretted leaving Hell for Earth now.

She decided to put the head out of its misery. She got out her gun, placed it on the head's left temple, then realized she wasn't alone.

The shadow of the vegan helicopter and the sound of its rotors presaged its appearance.

Morphia abandoned her thoughts of killing the head and ducked her hoverbike out of sight before it appeared over the ruintops.

She watched confused, as Death, 666, and the aug zombinators disembarked from it.

Able hadn't pissed off the veggie heretics too had he?

She parked her bike out of sight and padded stealthily across to spy on the vegan posse.

#

Using a metal detector, it took exactly one minute and twelve seconds to discover where Able and the womancows had carefully concealed their hoverbikes.

"Two bikes," 666 noted. "Only one was reported stolen by the farm guards."

Death nodded. "They had outside help then."

"Maybe the warden herself. Part of a conspiracy."

"Most likely."

She nodded to one of the zombinators. "Load these bikes into our copter." She turned back to 666. "They've clearly climbed the tree."

"Clearly." He pointed. "They left the ladder down."

"We go up after them."

"Most definitely."

They returned to their helicopter. It lifted and started ascending the lemon tree.

#

Keeping an eye on them, Morphia padded her way back to where she'd left her bike. She was intrigued by this new information that Able wasn't alone.

Able was climbing? So was she. With Necro's help...

The telltale cramps hit her then. Then again, her belly clenching like she'd been sucker-punched.

Morphia winced. Shit! Not here and not now. Please fuck no. But she *was* about starting her period. She'd had the signs for days now, been low-threshold irritable, but... she'd assumed her jumpiness was due to the stress of coordinating recent military operations.

She'd laid her simmering ill-humor at the door of Able's stupidity. The symptoms of Asshole Boyfriend Syndrome didn't differ greatly from those of PMS.

She felt a spurt at the top of her vagina, then the slightest trickle of blood on the passage's walls.

She cursed. In her hurry to leave, she'd not packed any sponge rats. Damn! This was stuff she could really do without now, particularly with that vegan helicopter also looking for Able.

Then she smirked. It didn't really matter--the little fuckers were everywhere in the worlderness, a veritable plague unto themselves.

She left the hoverbike and started rooting through the creepers smothering the ruins for rat holes.

#

Two minutes later she found what she was seeking, a moss-shrouded opening littered with oval pellets--rat droppings.

Morphia rolled up her sleeve and stuck her hand into the hole. She had to sink her arm elbow-deep into the building's foundation before feeling what she sought: A mass of furry terrified bodies, scampering to and fro to escape her questing fingers.

She closed her hand over the furry mass, ignoring the pain of their bites as they struggled to free themselves.

She pulled her hand out. She'd caught two. She broke the backs of both, then stuck her hand back into the hole to catch a couple more.

Finally she had eight rats, enough for three days--two if her flow was heavy. The paralyzed rats twitched pitifully, their glossy black beady eyes pleading with Morphia for mercy.

Sponge rats had to be used alive for best absorbance. Once dead, their pores contracted and their reservoirs held only a third of their full capacity.

More preparation remained now before they could be used as tampons.

Using her knife, Morphia broke all the rats' teeth out of their mouths so they couldn't bite her cunt. Then she cut off all their paws.

She smiled. Pussy hygiene was attended to. The discomfort she could cope with, the mess... no.

She pulled down her trousers and swiped her cunt opening with a finger--it came away red. She was just in time. She could feel additional streams of blood navigating her cervix.

She picked up one of the paralyzed sponge rats and after squeezing it to ensure it was dry, parted her labia and shoved it head-first up her cunt.

She pushed it in *deep*, till its rear legs had vanished and all that projected from her body was an inch of scaly tail-tip, just enough to extract the rat-tampon for disposal when it was soaked full of blood.

She pulled her pants back up, gathered up the rest of the rats, and returned to her bike.

*Time to climb*, she thought, unpacking her bone swords and strapping them to her back.

She walked over to the tree and began climbing also.

# Chapter 4

Able and his companions reached the next platform without incident. This was a hundred meters above the first.

Before slumping to rest, they took time to search-walk around the tree, ensuring there weren't any more were-zombies lurking.

"We can't keep climbing like this," Soil said.

"We won't," Able said. "That were-zombie clearly came from somewhere, a tunnel into the tree--a cuntdoor."

"I thought cuntdoors only existed at ground level," 219 said. She was eating the zombie intestines she'd draped herself with. They were intertwined with her foliage like snakes. Zombie juice dripped over her teeth.

Soil cut herself a slice of were-zombie liver and chewed on it slowly.

"The world's throwing up surprises at the moment," Able said. "I thought trees never grew this high." He sighed. "The only way the werewolf zombie could have gotten here was through a cuntdoor--those link directly to Hell. So there *must* be some on this tree."

"We should have checked around down there," Soil said, "instead of panicking."

"We're still panicking," 219 retorted. "This is just a brief interlude between bouts of fright and flight."

"Speak for yourself. I'm simply wisely removing my body from a succession of areas of danger."

Able left the conversation to them. 219 was right: This was a brief interlude between bouts of running, and he was personally already tired out. 219 was too. Only Soil seemed untired, like she was a flesh machine. It was a question for later.

(Soil's enhanced genes had kicked in once her discomfort level crossed a threshold set in Dr. October's lab--his built-in failsafe making her a reusable meatfield. Her body was now in turn leeching energy from the potatoes leeching energy from her, and using it to anesthetize her against their pain.

She felt this pain/counter-pain as an *unpleasant* vigor, a poisoned strength bubbling from a well within herself.

219 was in agony but hid it behind gritted teeth. She was keeping herself going by sheer willpower; by holding her desire to be more than mere farmland foremost in her mind.)

Able peered out between the leaves covering the platform edge. Yes, the damn chopper *was* rising towards them. Its progress was slowed by its continuous search for them as it lifted.

It would have metal detectors onboard.

He had a lot of metal stuff in his bag. No way was he going to escape detection.

He got out the brainshit tank from his bag and got to work making bombs from its contents.

#

Brainshit = human brains + human shit + mix together in the right proportions.

A lethally explosive mixture.

The necros, however, had never been able to get the proportions right, were reliant on what they stole from the vegans.

Able suspected there was a catalyst of some sort involved in the combination--possibly even bacteria resident in the bodies of the vegans themselves.

He scooped the brown brainshit putty out of the fuel tank and molded it.

There was enough for four bombs-- sufficient to take out one helicopter if judiciously used.

He made fuses from zombie thread pulled from his jacket, then checked that he had enough matches.

He pointed up, at a wide branch ten meters overhead. The branch both touched the ladder and extended out a short distance from the tree. "Time to throw our vegan guests a surprise party," he told the womancows.

Leaving the brainshit tank as metal detector bait, Soil, 219, and Able climbed up to the branch and lay in wait.

#

The helicopter arrived on cue, slow and inexorable as a bird of prey. Its rotors spun dizzily beneath them as it paused. Its metal sensors zeroed in on the abandoned fuel tank.

"They're here," Death said, lifting a hand from the controls to point. "There's a platform behind the leaf cover."

"We go in then," 666 said. He nodded to the zombinators.

Grappler hands at the ready, the augmented zombies moved to the helicopter's side doors as Death flew the chopper in closer to the tree.

#

Able nodded to Soil and 219 as the helicopter hovered below them, almost in touching distance of its propellers.

He lit all four bomb fuses, watched them sputter wickedly. "Remember, no misses. You two aim for the windscreen, I'll aim behind the propeller.

They dropped the bombs just as the zombinators were about to fire their grappler hands.

Three bombs hit directly on the helicopter. Soil's hit it on its front tip, below the cockpit. Both of Able's hit behind its propeller, blowing the aircraft's tail off.

The fourth...

"Have some brainshit you vegan shitheads, straight from my mental asshole like grandma--"

Attempting to drop her bomb, 219 overbalanced and fell off the branch, direct into the whirling propeller.

Soil and Able winced as she was chopped to leafy/meaty bits and spat in all directions by the propeller. Chunks of her brains hit two zombinators in the face. Both blew up and fell out of the helicopter.

Still clutching her bomb, 219's hand was flung ground-ward. Both loudly disintegrated seconds later.

The zombies fired their grappler hands at the tree. With the helicopter now spinning off balance, only one succeeded in hooking the edge of the platform.

Death fought to regain control of the helicopter. Her efforts were useless, however. The bombs had done too much damage.

The propeller stopped spinning. The vegan helicopter stuttered in midair for a second. Then it fell to earth in an agonizingly slow drop.

The zombie who'd snared the platform edge was wrenched from the falling machine and left dangling in midair.

Death, 666 and the three remaining zombinators fell with the machine, down to the world far below.

#

Able turned to Soil. "I'm truly sorry 'bout your friend," he said. "That'll take care of the zombies for awhile though.

Soil postponed her sadness over 219's death till later.

She pointed. "There's a zombie hanging on the tree. Let's get the fucker."

#

The dangling zombinator was winching himself over the edge of the platform when Able and Soil arrived by it.

Able shot him in the head. He disappeared over the side of the platform again, his metal arm unraveling. His grappler hand remained embedded in the platform.

"He'll be back up in a moment," Able said. "Those heretics are unstoppable--his skeleton's been replaced by metal. We need to dislodge this grapple-hook."

They both bent to the platform edge and began trying to work the metal claws free of the wood.

The zombie's left hand reappeared over the edge of the platform before they could do so.

"Here he comes again," Able said. He raised his gun again.

"Don't shoot," Soil said. "I've an idea."

She stepped up close to the platform edge just as the zombinator's head cleared it again. "You're coming back to the farm with me, womancow," he growled.

"Have some brains, fool," Soil said. She squatted and rubbed her cunt quickly in the zombinator's face as he pulled himself over the edge. Then she jumped back and watched his head explode from contact with the brain residue snagged in her cunt zip.

The zombie disappeared over the edge again and didn't reappear.

"I wasn't really sure that would work," Soil said.

Able looked over the edge of the platform. The zombinator's headless body dangled twenty feet below, swinging desolately. Its arms and legs clawed the air like they were still under conscious control.

"It worked all right," Able said. "Let's get the hell out of here.

# Chapter 5

Morphia climbed.

She heard the explosions overhead. A moment later the wrecked helicopter fell past her, flames spurting from it, its occupants helpless.

*Goodbye heretic fucks*, she thought, relieved that her bounty-hunting competition had been taken care of.

Killing Able would be her own personal conquest. His head would hang in the Temple of Undeath, an explicit lesson to any other blasphemers who sought to harness the holy writings for selfish ends.

She was impressed. Whoever Able had with him was tough, taking out a helicopter like that.

Irritatingly for one so much in a hurry, Morphia was forced to pause regularly during her climb.

Period pain she was used to coping with. The problem was her anus, still tender from her bone-fuck of two nights ago. The constant rubbing together of her buttock cheeks was no help at all.

#

She reached the platform where Able and the womancows had been attacked by the zombie werewolf.

*Shit*, she thought on seeing its remnants, still twitching in undead life, *Able really did a number on your ass.*

The smell of lemons hung heavy in the air. Morphia kicked fallen yellow fruit as she walked over to the excavated body.

Were-zombies existed in purity. Their flesh gave strength not harm to the eater. So read the Book of Undeath. Morphia cut herself a chunk of kidney and ate it. The rotting meat was delicious.

She turned the body over and sliced off a long strip of meat from waist to shoulder, carefully parting the worm-squirming musculature from its bone support. Extra food for the hunt.

She heard snuffling sounds.

She spun to her feet, knife hand extended.

*Shit, I overstayed my welcome.* Five more were-zombies had appeared from the other side of the tree trunk (where, as Able had supposed, there *was* a cuntdoor).

Morphia surveyed the hulking upright vulpine shapes with horror. Their dog-snouts, bristling with stinking white hair, and their hair-covered bodies, covered in turn by large hairless expanses--open sores in which maggots played like unsleepy toddlers.

Their red eyes like pools of jellied blood.

Their claws.

Their hungry open mouths with fangs ready to rip her apart and eat her.

These were Hell-spawn, impervious to brains and bullets--true beings of the food cycle.

*Eat zombie and be eaten.* The liturgy flooded her like a spring. She almost gave in to the blessedness of death here, to the temptation of achieving nirvana in the bellies of these true creatures of Necro.

Her warrior spirit rejected her death in such fashion. She was *necros*, also a blessed creature of God, constantly seeking to fulfill his will. She was on a mission now to destroy one who sought to destroy God's perfect order. Her sense of duty demanded that she fight and kill these things, blessed though they were.

She dropped her knife, and in a fluid motion, unsheathed the bone swords strapped to her back.

"Come to mommy," she told the were-zombies, swinging her blades. "Mommy will send you back to Hell."

#

The were-zombies circled and attacked Morphia. Their expectation of an easy kill was quickly cut short, however. Moving like lightning, she sliced and hacked at them with her swords.

She ducked out of the way of the first one that leapt at her, tripping it so it overbalanced over the platform edge.

It disappeared from sight in a howl of dismay.

With a double strike, Morphia sliced both of a were-zombie's arms off at its shoulders. It stood looking perplexed at its limbs wiggling about around its feet.

That took care of two. Three to go.

She skewered a third were-zombie through with her left sword, while slicing a fourth's arm off at the elbow with her right.

This move proved her undoing. The were-zombie she'd skewered didn't back off. It forced itself against her, clamping its jaws hard down on her left shoulder, like that which had attacked Able had done.

She couldn't get her left sword out of its body, so she left it and felt for her gun. She raised the sword in her right hand to skewer it through the neck, then felt her forearm caught by the jaws of the zombie werewolf whose arm she'd just truncated.

She got her gun out, but before she could raise it, the jaws of the armless were-zombie closed hard over the rear of her head, crumpling her skull and brain to mush as easily as if it was wet paper.

Blood exploded from her bald scalp like her assassin's tattoos were peeing red urine.

Morphia was dead even before the were-zombie biting her shoulder shifted its jaws and ripped her throat out.

Like she was participating in a group grope session, her corpse stood upright, braced against the skewered were-zombie, while they ate her, licking off the dripping brain goo that had spurted from her shattered skull onto her shoulders and jacket with their long doggy tongues.

# Chapter 6

Seated in meditation in his shrine in the holy hut, Priest felt Morphia's passing immediately when it happened. A deep chill dropped on him, coming seemingly from everywhere and nowhere at the same time.

Tears dripped down his fat face.

He wept both for his lost love and for the knowledge that now, only Necro himself could save the world from whatever Able Kane planned to do.

Priest *knew* that Morphia had died a blessed death at the hands of God's creatures. The knowledge was little comfort, knowing the horror that might shortly follow.

"Oh, Necro," he wept. "Save your faithful. May we not ourselves become that which we dread and hate the most--instruments of Hereticos."

He finished his purification and went to stand in the door of the holy hut. He stared into the distance, towards Texas, where the long thin line linking Earth and Haeven had appeared this morning.

Surely this too wasn't also Able Kane's doing?

Around him, the reconstruction of Death Raft 4 was well underway. The necros dead would have their brains extracted and their bodies buried, after both Neck's beds here and in the Temple had been replenished with meat, of course.

Huts were being rebuilt and engines and flooring repaired.

The candidates from the last village for admission into the necros were hard at work, helping rebuild.

Priest grimaced at the huge distant lemon tree, wondering what it was.

He was long past regretting his failed attempt to rid himself of his pet heretic. Who was to say Able Kane's escape, occurring fortuitously at the same time as the vegan attack, wasn't fated by Necro himself?

If such was the case, Morphia had died for nothing.

Feeling deeply angry with Necro for the first time he could remember, Priest turned back into the holy hut.

#

In their bedroom, Neck waited like a time bomb. Priest was dismayed to see her erection. It throbbed like a vegan antigrav engine. Surely not now?

"Yes, *now*, Priest," Neck said, reading his thoughts. "I too have sensed her passing. This is the cleansing of her soul."

Priest stalled, indicating their chained concubines. "But surely, one of the harem."

"No. This cleansing must be performed by we who loved her."

Priest nodded. One didn't argue with God. He climbed into the meat bed.

And it was true. He felt reassurance return as they caressed each other, felt his anger against Necro fade into his subconscious again, till he was unsure why he'd been so angry to begin with. True the world might end from one heretic's foolishness, but the world had ended twice before, and now Necro would recreate it in his image.

"In her image," Neck said.

"Huh?"

"Turn over. I want to be the man. This is the highest point of communion."

Priest turned over. He relaxed his body. He relaxed his asshole as he felt Neck slide her meat-juice slickened dick up inside him.

It felt good today, to have all responsibility taken from him.

*God is in my anus,* he thought, *all is well with Earth.*

He relaxed and floated on the rotten meat, its stench aphrodisiac to his senses. His cock was hard like the bones in the meat he was fucking in turn as she fucked him, forcing his erection into the smooth yielding tunnels it made in the packed flesh.

He came and came again into the decay. Blessed release for one loved.

Neck fucked Priest long and hard. When she felt the buildup of her cum-maggots in her balls, she wrapped both her hands tightly around his neck and began throttling him.

Priest was sleepy by then, weakened from a trio of orgasms, the like he'd rarely had.

He only realized Neck was killing him when she forced his head deep into the bed, cutting off his air.

No! He choked on coagulated blood. He fought to free himself from the cock in his ass and the weight of her body, but she was too strong for him.

He died as she came into his ass, an ejaculation of maggots that forced her cock out of his body with their sheer profusion.

Neck rolled off Priest's corpse, and frowned. This was the hardest she'd fucked in a long time, and she was tired. But it had felt very good.

She wiped the milk-white larvae off her thighs. Then she climbed out of bed and put on Priest's robe of zombie faces. She left the bedroom and walked to the door of the holy hut, then out into the evening sun.

It was time to begin the kingdom of Haeven on Earth. With Morphia not returning, there was no one to oppose her ascension.

#

The necros' shock at seeing their xombina God walk amongst them openly for the first time quickly turned to worshipful adoration.

A group of underpriests made a delegation and bowed to her. The rest of the people followed suit.

"My lord," one said, "we don't understand."

"Priest is dead. He will be made part of my meat bed and as so will be a part of me forever."

"Yes, Lord, it will be done," the priests said. "Who is priest now?"

The xombina indicated her robe of faces.

"*I* am Priest now," she said. "I will lead you to the promised land." She paused to let her words sink in, then added: "For too long have the decrees of the great Necro been diluted by being transmitted through human flesh. I am the new Priest, pure and holy, eating meat as decreed by Necro. You all will heed me."

Neck knew that she gambled. There was the very real chance that despite Morphia's absence, the necros would reject her headship and demand the continuation of the previous order. But no, the necros were too conditioned by generations of ingrained belief to question either her godhood or its decreed pre-emptive prerogative.

She frowned at the priests. "We waste time here. It is time I inspect my temple, and teach the evening worship of I."

The kneeling priests got to their feet.

"Priest is dead," they chanted as one, as the liturgy demanded when a new ruler was crowned. "Long live Priest."

"Long live Priest," the multitudes chanted back.

# Chapter 7

Death picked herself off the floor and looked around.

She was standing at the bottom of a deep crater.

She ensured she wasn't broken anywhere, dusted herself off, then climbed up to its rim and looked around.

Helicopter wreckage was strewn around as far as she could see.

She looked up at the tree.

Those bastards!

Being Death meant never dying and rarely being seriously damaged. Zombies were the same where dying was concerned. Their rotten flesh kept living even in the house bricks of the necros.

They were, however, far from indestructible. That was cause for concern now for Death. *666!*

She began searching the area for her lover and the other zombinators.

#

Of the three zombies who had been in the crashed helicopter, one had been decapitated by a propeller blade.

The remaining two, a male and female, were in good shape. Both had large tears in their bodies through which their reinforced steel skeletons were visible.

Both had dents in their heads, meatless craters revealing their metal skulls.

In addition, Boris, the male zombie, had lost his right eye.

"Where's 666?" Death asked.

"Over here." The zombinator pulled himself out of a building roof and dropped to the ground beside them. Being more armor plated than the others, he'd suffered less damage.

They looked up at the tree again.

"That didn't work," Blueteeth, the female zombinator said.

Death looked at her sharply, her knife-wound mouth set in a frown. "No it didn't."

"We climb instead," 666 said, turning and heading for the lemon tree again.

Part Five:
Hellcome to Haeven

# Chapter 1

On the sixth platform up, Able and Soil saw their first cuntdoor.

"So *this* is what a hellpussy looks like," Soil said.

The cuntdoor was a monster upright-oval opening framed with vine tendrils. Since this was a lemon tree, its natural fishy odor was mingled with citrus fragrance, the result smelling like the DEZA queen had just douched.

The cockrocket, stuck halfway to its testicles in the door, was a huge white-metal vehicle, longer than a hoverbus.

Above its testicles it had two side fins and a large tail fin.

Behind these, it had four circular engines, all blackened with soot, like the cockrocket had crash-landed into the cuntdoor.

The rocket had a row of reinforced glass windows along the upper fuselage on each side.

Painted on its top tail fin was an emblem: A rectangle of horizontal white and red lines; along with a smaller blue rectangle, featuring fifty white stars in its top left corner.

Below the emblem was writing. Able read it off:

"'NASA Space Program: Space Shuttle; Launch from Cape Canaveral'."

"Who in zombie's withered anus are NASA?" Soil asked. "The fucking vegans again?"

Able nodded. "Ancient ones. From before the re-creation."

#

Able and Soil finally stopped ascending the lemon tree between the tenth and eleventh platform up.

Beside the ladder was a brown door, cunningly concealed so it looked like a chunk of loose bark.

"We stop here," Able said, locating the door's handle, disguised as a twig. "I'm done with climbing. "We enter *here*."

"We should go up a little higher," Soil said. "I think--"

"Forget it," Able interrupted, "it's not happening. This is the first door we've reached that isn't a cuntdoor. We've no idea how long it'll be before we reach another."

"We've surely missed several before this one."

"We're sure to miss another several after this."

Soil nodded. "Okay." It was strange to her that Able was so tired. She had no reason to refuse entering the tree except that she felt strong and bursting with life. Even the 'poisoned' feeling earlier, dampening her reinvigoration, had since dissolved into intense inexplicable wellbeing.

She felt able to ascend to the top of the world if need be.

#

They opened the door and entered a city street. Except that it was somewhat better maintained, they could still be in Texas.

They stepped through onto crumbling stone.

"What's it say?" Soil asked, pointing to the green/white sign that faced them, nailed to the side of a house like a street name.

Able sighed. "It says 'Welcome to Haeven'."

"The home of Necro? God? The top of the world?"

"One and the same." He looked back out through the door they'd just entered, (which was now the front door of a totally gutted bus), to the leafy boughs of the tree, and the peeks of sky beyond them. "You were right, this isn't anywhere to be. Let's keep climbing."

Soil shook her head. "No point." She pointed to the wide opening five meters to their right through which a thick crest of foliage poked. Dangling from its topmost branches were huge ripe lemons. "This is where the tree leads."

"Yeah," Able said. He shut the door and sat on the sidewalk. "Welcome to Haeven."

#

"This place is the absolute shits," Able said. "You'd think God would keep his domain in better repair."

They were walking the streets, seeking somewhere to hide.

"Yeah," Soil agreed. She spat in the ankle-high dust.

"We should be able to lose ourselves here," Able said. "At least that's..."

He stopped speaking as a half-decayed man shambled into view. Both ducked out of sight through an empty doorway.

"A zombie," Soil whispered.

"Not the sort we're familiar with," Able whispered back. "Look!"

The zombie shambled down the street, walking like it was underwater. As it neared their place of concealment, two more zombies, one male, one female, shambled into view at the top of the street, each seemingly more decayed than the other. Both walked with the same slow-motion tread of the first. All three zombies had eaten-away faces through which their teeth showed, and eyes swollen like pregnancies.

"What's wrong with them?" Soil asked.

"Nothing. They're the original zombies as Necro designed them to be: The blessed glorious ones."

"They look like shit. The ones on the farm look better."

Able hid his anger at her blasphemy. This stupid womancow had a lot to learn.

The first zombie passed them by.

"Brainssss!" it whispered. "Brainssss!!!" It turned and saw them, but didn't stop. "Brainnnsssssss! Brainssss!!!"

"That's odd, Able," Soil said. "Why would a zombie be calling for brains?"

Able agreed. Why indeed? "Something's wrong here."

The other two zombies passed them, also calling for brains.

"That's real odd," Able said.

Then he heard it, a loud stomping sound.

"That doesn't sound good," he told Soil.

The source of the sound came into view. It was a monster *brain*, twice as high as Able and proportionately long. It lumbered on a pair of short legs projecting from its undersurface. Its front lobes were a series of lips splitting the surface of its head into many convoluted mouths.

Behind the first came six of other giant brains.

"Eat zombies!!!" the brains rumbled as they trod through the dusty road after the fleeing zombies.

Able looked at Soil. "Are you *really* sure you don't want us to go back and start climbing the tree again?"

She shook her head. "I like it here. Nice to be somewhere where the zombies aren't dangerous. Besides, we're safe here."

Able didn't share her confidence. From what he knew of zombinators, they were very hard to kill. They were certain to have survived that horrendous crash of close to a mile, and already be climbing up the tree again.

They had the edge in time, however. He doubted the zombies would find the door they'd come here through. Hopefully the heretical shits would climb all the way to the top of the tree. Or even mistakenly enter a cuntdoor.

He said nothing of his doubts and worries to his womancow companion.

Soil watched happily as the seven pursuing brains caught up with the fleeing zombies. She pulled a piece of were-zombie from her cuntbag and chewed it while she watched the brains savage the somnolent undead, ripping them apart, throwing chunks of them into the air and wolfing them down wholesale into the many mouths rippling their surfaces.

She was enjoying herself. It was nice to see zombies on the receiving end of a rain of shit for a change.

"Those are the oddest creatures I've ever seen," Able said. "The holy scriptures don't mention carnivorous brains anywhere."

"Those aren't the sort of brains we have," Soil replied to him. "They're not like human brains at all."

"Huh?"

She wiped her mouth clean of meat with a leafy hand before explaining. "Yeah, the zombies aren't exploding on contact with them, like they would human brains."

Able considered that a moment. "Maybe they're celestial brains--divine brains."

#

Able's original plan had been to move to the town's opposite side, as far away from the hole in the road through which the top of the lemon tree poked.

"If we do that," Soil pointed out, "we'll have no way of knowing when the zombinators get here."

Able conceded the truth of that. They set up temporary quarters in a house in clear view of both the bus and the treetop.

All through that day the huge brains hunted zombies up and down their street, neither group paying them any heed. The street was soon strewn with tatters of zombie clothing, hair, and skin scraps fallen from the brains' mouths.

Finally, Soil concluded the obvious.

"We're safe up here. Even those zombinators can't fight brains this huge."

"They'll try anyway. Let's wait till tomorrow before moving out."

## Chapter 2

The next morning Able found he had a new problem.

He was woken by the sound of Soil groaning in pain. He sat up in alarm. Thinking they'd been attacked, he trained his gun on her, then away from her to the doorway.

"There's no one in the room," Soil whimpered from where she lay on the floor, rolling side to side in utter agony. "It's me. I'm ripe."

Able rushed to her side and saw she was right. Her leaves were smeared with blood. He stuck a hand between her neck leaves, her body was slippery. His hand came away red.

*Shit.*

"I don't understand this," Soil whimpered. "I've only been on the vegfarm for two years. I've still three to go before my blood potatoes ripen."

"Maybe the stress of your escape caused it," Able said. He was thinking of the bottle of pink liquid in his bag. He could try his cure on her.

Soil misinterpreted his distracted look.

"Help me, you son of a bitch: I'll die if I don't get rid of these shitty things."

"You'll die if you do," Able said. "You know that."

"Just do something--*anything*. This pain is driving me out my mind." Gone now was all feeling of transcendent vigor, the sense that she could take on the world single-handed. She clenched her teeth as the blood potatoes in her scalp fed impulses through her nerves. It felt like her head was splitting into two.

"Fuck you, Able!" she screamed, as her body felt like it was being quartered. "Just do fucking something! Fucking Kill me! Kill me!! KILL ME!!!!"

"No need to go to that extreme," Able said quietly. He crossed the room to his bag and got out his cure.

"Open your mouth," he said. "This won't hurt."

She sputtered the pink liquid up, then swallowed it down. She lay back down, clutching her sides and moaning.

"Shouldn't take more than five minutes," Able said gently. "Hang in there. You'll be fine soon."

He wasn't sure she would. All he'd experimented on were limbs smuggled into his hut-lab when Morphia was out--arms and legs from humans captured/killed in raids.

Blood potatoes had been easy to come by. Every sacked zombie settlement had stocks of them.

Then he saw her leaves were withering, and breathed a sigh of relief.

Soil yawned. "I feel sleepy," she said. She lifted her hand to her eyes and saw she no longer had leaves. She sat up, watched her vines also dissolve off her flesh, leaving her naked for the first time since she could remember.

She looked at Able in wonder. "You really did it." She frowned, studying the multitude of tuber bumps dotting her body. "The potatoes are still in me--though I don't hurt anymore." She peered at him expectantly. "I look horrible. Can you get them out?"

Able shook his head. This was the hard part to explain. "They won't come out," he said. "They're changing inside you. You're changing too, the medicine changes you. You'll see what I mean in a moment."

Soil felt the change start. She looked at her hands, saw they'd turned bright pink and fleshy. Her skin glimmered like the inner surface of a lip.

Her multitude of potato bumps popped their surfaces and through the holes sprouted large white extrusions.

Soil gaped. There was something disturbingly familiar about the shape of the extrusions.

Able stared unhappily at her as he explained. "That's the catch--what I couldn't fix. The cure turns your body tissue into mouth gum tissue.

Soil got the point. She stared at the large white projections now jutting out all over her body. Some were six inches long and curved and sharp, other shorter and dull edged. She gaped at him in horror. "I'm growing *teeth*. You turned my blood potatoes to fucking *teeth*?"

Able attempted a smile then gave up. "I couldn't just let you die, could I?"

Soil stood looking at Able in disbelief while her gum-skin's teeth each grew out to their full lengths.

\#

"Some fucking cure," Soil said angrily.

"Most important is that it works," Able said defensively. "You're the living proof. Remember, that's the key word--*Living*. You're *alive*." He sighed. "Look, I'm sorry about the side effects, but you admitted yourself, you feel great."

This was true--she did feel fantastic, even more so than when climbing the tree. "So? I still look like shit."

Able stared her down angrily. "And what did you look like before? I'll tell you--a tree that was going to die. Can't see a huge amount of difference from where I'm standing. Except that you're still alive."

"Thanks," Soil said drily. "I still don't like being covered in teeth."

"You *should be* thankful. There's more: You're potato-proof now, even if the zombies could get the teeth out of your body, it won't grow blood potatoes anymore.

"That's small comfort."

"Try to be grateful. I got chased out of the necros for this."

"*For this?* Why?" She read the answer in his sullen look. "You told them it was possible to cure the humancows on the farms, and starve the vegans into extinction? So what was the problem?"

Able shook his head sadly. "I apparently got a little carried away during my pharmaceutical presentation. Said too much. Being in God's presence does that to you."

"*God?*"

Able sighed. "Little womancow..." he began patronizingly. Then he laughed. "No you're not that anymore--you eat zombies like a true believer. Soil Woman, religion is a complicated, complicated business. You're never sure if you're right doubting it, or wrong believing it. For ages I thought everyone was better off without it, but then I met Neck and my faith in zombie was renewed."

"Who's Neck? God's throat?"

"*Neck*... not neck. The personification of God in flesh. The completion of the male-female principle in zombie."

He saw that she didn't understand. He got out his copy of the Book of Undeath, and explained the holy writings to her.

#

Afterwards, they sat in the doorway watching the brains chase and eat the zombies again.

"It's just the teeth," Soil said. "I feel really great otherwise."

"It might be possible to extract them, just like normal teeth," Able said. "Or file them down so they don't show. Once I've spread this cure in the vegfarm waters, we'll have enough--"

"You're really going to give everyone body-teeth like me? Able, think for Necro's sake."

Able smiled at her reference to the true god. "I *have* thought," he said grimly. "And I *think* looking odd's a lot better than dying at the hands of vegan heretics."

He got to his feet, extended his hand to her. "Let's go for a walk, look the town over. We'll move from here tomorrow if the zombinators haven't shown up."

#

He woke that night to find Soil masturbating. She lay on her back, raised off the ground by her body-teeth, and was sliding her cuntbag's zip fastener back and forth with motions of increasing rapidity, moaning like she was possessed by Necro.

Able smiled. She really was cured-- humancows had zero libido. He lay back down discreetly and waited till she'd come with her orgasm of violent spasms.

#

By next morning, however, Able saw that his cure hadn't gone all according to plan.

Soil looked MUCH different.

"I feel fantastic," she said. "Totally killer."

*You look killer,* he thought.

Her formerly slick and moist gum-skin had now hardened. Able was sure the thin lines crisscrossing her body marked the beginnings of scales.

Her legs, her thighs in particular, were now thrice as thick as they'd been.

In addition, her face had begun elongating into a snout, and her teeth were taking on the aspect of those of a carnivore, like those of the were-zombie they'd killed.

He wondered for a moment if it wasn't an infection from eating the zombie werewolf's flesh. He rejected the idea. Nowhere in the scriptures was there mention of such a curse. Also, she'd shown no such signs till he'd fed her his cure.

More worrying of all the changes in her, however, was the fact that she now towered over him by a foot. Her body-teeth had grown proportionately, though spacing out with the expansion of her body. There was a definite crest of molars running from the nape of her neck to her... he caught himself just before he thought 'tail.' He couldn't deny the fleshy twitching extension riding just above the cleft in her buttocks.

Soil noticed his concerned look. "Are you all right?" Her voice was slightly slurred, slightly growly.

"It's you I'm concerned about," he replied.

"Don't worry, I'm fine," Soil said airily.

*That*, the blithe lack of concern over these additional and extreme distortions of her body, from a woman who'd yesterday been irate over a much lesser alteration, worried Able most of all.

Clearly Soil was transforming into something he'd not planned or intended.

He made a fire and roasted the were-zombie meat she extracted from her cuntbag.

They ate and set out.

For a long moment, Able considered ending his hopes/plans of human salvation there and then. He took out his bottle of pink liquid, and looked at it, then looked at the giant Soil, smiling benevolently down at him.

*Smash it!* one voice screamed in his head.

*Do that and all hope's lost forever,* the opposing mental advocate yelled back. *Side effects or no, it's the only cure there is. The only humancow hope.*

Confused, Able Kane stuck his bottle of liquid back into his bag.

He smiled wearily at Soil and they set out.

# Chapter 3

Death and the zombinators reached the blood-splattered platform and stared at Morphia's remains--mostly cracked bones strewn everywhere like fruit seeds. Departing the platform after eating her, the were-zombies had removed both their own severed limbs and the headless corpse of the one killed by Able Kane.

Blueteeth, the female zombinator, plucked a lemon and examined it.

"Too bad blood potatoes don't grow on trees," her male counterpart, Boris, said.

"Too bad indeed," 666 agreed. "Then we could kill off the disgusting humans once and for all."

He spoke out of fear. Despite his massive size, 666 shared the pedestrian zombie's instinctive terror of brains. It was something he'd never shared with anyone. Staring now at the goo smears that had once filled Morphia's head, he felt the stacked weight of generations of zombie horrors press on him.

Death picked up one of Morphia's bone swords. "Their helpers are necros," she said. "This is their workmanship."

"The necros are scavengers, humancows the garbage they root through," 666 said. "It's a fitting pairing."

"Shall we search for the animal which killed this one?" Boris asked.

"No," 666 replied. "The longer we wait the farther away they get. They attacked us farther up, below an overhanging branch."

Death agreed. "We keep climbing."

"I recall something," Blueteeth said. "During the explosions, a womancow fell into the propellers and was killed."

"Yes," 666 said. "Her face fell through the propellers and past me. I saw her ID number. She was 219f, not the one Dr. October needs."

"So we now track only one humancow," Boris said.

"And her helpers," Death added. "Don't forget them." She indicated Morphia's bones. "This one *didn't* attack us, so there's still at least one more necros at large."

They started up the ladder again.

#

They passed the headless zombinator, still swinging to and fro at the end of his winch-arm.

"Keep going," 666 said. "He is beyond help."

#

They paused again at the second platform.

Death pointed to Able's empty brainshit fuel tank. "That's what deceived us."

In a sudden flash of white lightning and a whirlwind motion the leaves parted and a zombie stood facing them.

He was seven feet tall and broad-shouldered, with chest and arm muscles even more hulking than 666's. His waist and legs were proportionately smaller but still powerfully built.

His skull was perforated with holes in and out of which crawled long blue worms that sparked with electricity.

His face was mostly skeleton. His eyes were expressionless eggs. His lips were rotted away. His skin and flesh existed on his frame in an exceptional stage of advanced decay. Gangrene stench poured from him like expensive cologne.

He was dressed in tight red shorts with 'SZ' painted over the crotch in white, with the 'S' designed to look like a reversed 'Z'.

Death felt a glow of admiration for the newcomer. He was powerfully sexy. In addition, there was something familiar about him, like they'd met before, only she couldn't remember where.

"Who... are you?" she asked. Her companions just kept staring at the new arrival.

"I am Superzombie," he said. "Stronger than your urge to puke at the sight of meat, faster than your death by brain contamination."

As he spoke he gesticulated with his hands. Both were hammy and huge, and like his headworms, crackled with electricity.

"I flew out here to investigate the appearance of this tree and heard you talking." He peered at them all in turn. "I am the defender of truth, justice and the modern zombie way of life. What are you doing here?"

"DEZA business," 666 said, preparing to fight. "Need to know basis..."

"And you *don't* need to know," Death finished for him.

For a moment there was tension in the air, with the zombinators all getting set to release their built-in body weaponry and Superzombie readying to attack and repulse them.

Then Superzombie smiled. "I respect the DEZA," he said. "Our great nation would be nothing without their strong leadership." He scratched his bone chin with a huge hand, electric sparks leaping from his fingertips to outline his teeth. "They throw many wasteful parties, but that is normal of leaders."

He nodded at them. "I leave. One of your number dangles headless from this platform. I will return him to Neo La. Maybe there is a head needing a body there."

"Yes, maybe," 666 agreed.

With that, Superzombie was gone. They had the briefest impression of him stepping backward off the platform and plummeting downwards. A moment later, he was visible as a gray streak in the sky, heading away from them at the speed of sound.

Only then did they realize Superzombie had somehow managed to unhook the dangling zombinator's hand from the platform edge while falling too fast for their eyes to keep track of him.

"Wow," Blueteeth said, watching him go. "That's one real cool zombie."

"Hey, let's get a move on!" 666 called testily.

#

Up, up, up, they passed without noticing Able Kane's and Soil's exit door from the tree.

On the next platform, 666 called a halt.

"We've passed six cuntdoors so far," he said. "They wouldn't dare enter those."

"No. They would be fucked and they know it. Cuntdoors lead only to Hell."

"So there must be other doors. We've climbed thrice as fast as any human could manage, particularly a ripe humancow. We'd otherwise have overtaken them by now."

"The doctor says this humancow is special--our equal even."

"Remember, she is not alone. Her necros partner would need to rest."

Death nodded. "So they went in somewhere."

She looked over at the cuntdoor in the tree--the one blocked by a cockrocket. *Surely not into one of these?*

This cockrocket's unburied rear body was violently warped. It was split into metal strips folded back on themselves, like a peeled banana. Broken metal rails projected from its inner surface like mechanical insect legs. Its testicle doors dangled at the end of these peeled-back segments like rusted bells on a clown's hat.

A melted steel door sealed off access both to the undestroyed anterior portions of the vehicle and the tree's interior.

The rocket's left lateral tail-fin was cracked off, its stars-and-stripes emblem and writing just distinguishable amidst layers of dust and rust.

"Who are NASA?" Boris asked, echoing Soil's earlier question to Able Kane.

"An ancient space race," Death replied, with a cryptic smile.

"I've heard rumors some cockrockets have skeletons in them," Blueteeth said. "Pilots and passengers."

"Yeah right," Boris said. "Believe that, you'll believe anything."

"Look," 666 said, "we must not digress into fables." He felt it imperative that they not sidetrack themselves from their objective. Their earlier encounter with Superzombie was sufficient distraction for today. "The womancow we're hunting didn't go through any of the cuntdoors we've passed. So we start looking for the door she *did* go through."

"Meaning we head back down," Death said, peering out through the leaves over the worlderness. "No way they climbed up this high."

# Chapter 4

Haeven extended forever. That was how it seemed to Able Kane.

They'd been walking through the streets for half a day now.

In that time, the number of undead walking the streets had tripled, as had the number of brains hunting them.

"I'll admit Haeven's a cuntball place, but..."

Able was becoming more worried about Soil's ongoing transformation by the minute. She was now hoverbus-sized and still growing in visible spurts.

Her skin was now brown armor-plate scales, her body-teeth huge yellow projections that ripped stone from walls she walked too close to.

Her head had become a reptile's--a sand-lizard's or snake's. It was as long as Able himself. Her teeth were foot-long scimitars.

Soil still walked upright for the most part, but was more regularly falling forward to walk on all fours, like an animal, just like she'd now taken to rearing up on her 'hind' legs (Able couldn't help the metaphor) and baying at the sun when the fancy took her.

Her ID '15f' was visible as raised 'block' writing on her forehead scales. Able didn't understand how that was possible. Just like he didn't understand how her cuntbag had grown along with the rest of her. Its zip-fastener dragged along behind her like an additional tail, below her actual tail.

And he didn't understand why she still seemed in such an overwhelmingly good mood.

#

Soil *was* in an overwhelmingly good mood. Animals lack the concerns of the average person, and she was fast becoming one.

She was, however, growing hungry, and unknown to Able, she'd begun thinking of him more as food than friend.

#

Almost like it had appeared out of a dream, they turned a corner and stumbled onto a huge plain.

"Huh?" Able said.

"Wow," Soil whispered down at him.

The sky above the plain thronged with the huge brains. Like untethered dirigibles, they floated to and fro, darkening the portions of Haeven beneath them.

Around the boundaries of the plain the town continued like normal.

"I think that's God's house," Soil said, pointing.

Able followed her claw. In the far distance stood a solitary building, a replica of the temple hut on Death Raft 4.

"Most likely," he agreed drily.

"We go visit him then?"

Able was immediately struck by a crisis of confidence. Meeting Necro, what would he ever say? Explain how he'd doubted his very existence till three days ago?

"Let's go visit God," Soil repeated. "He might be glad to see us."

"Okay," he grudgingly agreed.

They set off across the plain.

#

The plain extended for miles and miles. It was dotted with zombie villages.

In between these villages were large expanses occupied mainly by smaller brains pursuing and killing zombies.

They reached two brains dangling a zombie between them, fighting over possession. One brain had the zombie's legs in two adjacent mouths, the other had the zombie's head in an upper mouth and arm in a lower. The pair grunted and growled and pulled forward and backwards in their tussle. Finally, the zombie ripped apart at the waist, spraying intestines everywhere.

Trailing body organs, each brain ran off, pursued by other brains seeking to steal the zombie meat.

"They're like dogs with bones," Able said.

They passed two brains screwing a headless female zombie.

They stopped to watch.

The brains had floppy three-foot-long penises that looked like spinal cords.

After they ejaculated into the xombina, she swelled and turned into a brain herself, her body fattening, her arms and legs shrinking to nothing, and her skin becoming moist and convoluted.

Finally her skeleton spurted out of her anterior lobe, convoluted mouths appearing in bits and pieces. She got up and joined the brains. The trio ran off looking for another zombie to fuck to undeath.

#

They passed many more scenes of brains raping zombies.

Male zombies didn't become brains when raped. They turned into slithering spinal cord creatures with hundreds of nerve legs. These nerve-centipedes in turn crawled atop the fucking and feeding brains and disappeared into holes in their rear surfaces.

#

In distant corners of the plain there were brains clustered so thick they looked like herds of clouds.

#

There were holes in the ground through which they could see the under-sky.

"This is totally fucked-up," Able said.

"Why? We climbed above the sky to get here. It's natural it should be under us now."

Able wished she'd stop being so blasé about everything. He stuck a hand through the hole, felt cold air currents swirl around his fingers.

Soil sat patiently watching him for a while. Then she got to her feet. "Stop fooling around, Able, let's go."

#

Halfway to the temple, the violence abruptly ceased, like an invisible line had been drawn across the plain.

On their side of it, brains filled the sky and plain, raping and eating zombies. On the other side of it a mob-thick throng of zombies shambled aimlessly back and forth with not a single brain in sight, either on earth or in sky.

"I think we've reached the core of Necro's influence," Able said.

Soil didn't reply.

He looked up at her. She'd been growing all the while they'd been crossing the plain. She was now twenty feet high and walked with the heavy tread of a mastodon. He'd started wondering if the ground would hold up to her weight, particularly if they walked over another holed patch unawares.

He saw she was looking down at him with an odd gleam in her eyes.

"I'm hungry, Able," she growled. "Must eat now!"

# Chapter 5

Soil had felt her hunger increasing as they approached the invisible wall. It built up inside her like her recent orgasm, instinct-wrenching control of her senses. She looked at the brains and zombies around her. None interested her. The brains smelled wrong and the zombies smelled rotten. There was one right smell and that was Able.

She looked down at Able.

He looked back up at her. "You can't eat these zombies," he said. "They aren't pure."

"Meat," Soil said. "But not zombie."

Able looked up sharply, uncertain he'd heard right. *"What?"*

"Human meat is good, pure for womancows."

"What?"

"I eat you, Able. Good pure meat."

Her huge jaws swung down towards him. Able ducked out of their way and ran. He realized she'd crossed the invisible barrier separating woman from beast, and he leapt through the invisible barrier into the mob of zombies.

Once he'd dashed ten zombies deep into the mob, he ducked down and crawled to his left.

Soil moved to stop him, then realized she couldn't see him. Her hunger gnawed her insides like termites eating wood. Food, food, FOOD!!! She stamped through the invisible barrier seeking Able.

She could smell him, but his exact location was masked by the horrible rotten zombie stench.

Maddened by hunger and frustration, Soil began stamping right and left, bending and swatting the zombie intrusions out of the way.

She was hungry, hungry, HUNGRY. EAT, EAT, EAT!!!

Able peeked up and saw the monstrous Soil throwing zombies through the air like she was raking leaves.

He ducked back down and kept making his way through the shiftless undead mob, no longer bothering to go sideways, just run-crawling on hands and knees as fast as he could go.

The zombies ended a hundred yards from the temple steps. At that point, they became a wall around the building, as though another invisible barrier prevented them from moving any closer to its divine holiness.

Crouched just outside this new separation, Able cursed Necro. There was no fucking way he was making it across that distance alive. Soil would cover it in ten steps once she spotted him. It would take him at least twenty-five.

And even if he made it, he couldn't guarantee she'd not follow him into the temple.

Then the light literally shone for him.

Through a patch of ground to the right of the steps he saw the blue under-sky. Then he saw another crack in the earth, then another, reaching back to ten meters from where he stood.

He smiled grimly. Do or die time this was.

He ran out over the weakened ground and turned to face Soil. He was surprised. She was scooping zombies into the sky so copiously it seemed she was juggling them in groups. Many were already broken and shredded by her claws as she trod through them looking for him.

Crazily to Able, those zombies she'd not harmed in her rampage, kept pacing like she wasn't even there.

She hadn't yet noticed Able standing out in the open. He was tempted to run for the temple, but stuck to his plan.

"Hey, Soil Monster!!!" he yelled. "I'm over he-eere!!!"

The multitude of confusing smells thinned to one for Soil.

*Able?*

Looking like a skyscraper come to life, she reared up and saw him. Her forehead ID was a set of ledges built into her flesh.

"I eat Able Kane!" Soil thundered, abandoning the zombies.

Stamping undead to undead mush, she raced at him.

#

Able ran immediately once he had her undivided attention. He ran straight over the weakened patch of Haeven's temple forecourt. He heard Soil's massive steps as she pounded after him, then her yelp of surprise.

Heaving a massive sigh of relief, he spun around.

Soil was stuck in the ground. She'd plunged waist-deep through the weakened earth.

Through a hole closer to him, Able saw her rear legs thrashing violently, trying to make purchase on thin air, only succeeding in pulling her deeper into the hole in the ground.

"Able!" she screamed. "EAT, EAT!"

"You've got to be crazy, woman," Able said. In dread, he watched her pound the ground in frustration, each horrendous blow shaking the dubious foundation of Haeven itself and widening the hole she was in.

Then the ground around her gave way totally, and she fell through.

Able sat down in relief, disbelieving his ears.

Soil was still screaming "EAT ABLE EATTTTTT!!!!" as she fell down to the worlderness below.

He sat shuddering for a long time. Then he picked up his bag and began the climb up the temple steps.

"Dumb crazy womancow bitch," he muttered angrily.

# Chapter 6

## *The valley of the Shadow of Brains*

Death and the zombinators found a non-cunt door, two tree-doors above that by which Soil and Able had entered Haeven.

Death pushed the door open and they entered.

"This is a nightmare," 666 muttered.

"A very horrible one," Blueteeth agreed, her voice edgy.

The zombinators had emerged in Haeven, on the same plain housing the temple of Necro.

In the near distance the skyscraper-sized Soil towered over everything.

The zombinators gaped at the huge brains everywhere. They were particularly shocked by those floating overhead.

Conquering their ingrained horror in the presence of brains, the three zombies held their guns ready for combat.

"Where are we?"

"I think Haeven," Death said.

"This can't be Haeven," Boris objected, "it must be Hell."

"I don't think our womancow's here," Death said. "Unless she's that monster over there."

"Cannot be," 666 said. "That is an ancient dinosaur."

They could see the commotion around Soil as she threw zombies into the air like confetti, but had no idea what she was doing. 666 nodded to his companion zombinators. "We're here--we search here to make sure she's not here. But be on your guard, that creature looks dangerous."

Then Soil fell through the ground. They watched patiently while she struggled her way down through the hole she'd made and disappeared from view.

"That's one less problem," 666 said. "Let's go."

"Be careful," Death added, "watch the ground for holes."

#

After proceeding a hundred meters they became aware that the huge brains, both overhead and around them were coming toward them at great speed. Before they could track backward, they were hemmed in on both sides, looking at the distant temple down an aisle of pale glimmering lobed flesh.

The overhead brains made the aisle almost a tunnel.

"Eat zombie," the brains screamed. For the first time they saw the series of convoluted mouths that formed each brain's front hemispheres--a wall of teeth extending above and beyond them.

"Eat zombie!!"

"They've ideas well above their station," Death said blithely. "Being oversized does that to you."

"This is bad trouble," Boris said. "They are too many."

"We aren't spineless humancows!" Blueteeth snarled at him. "We are the zombinators--elite zombie troops!"

"Better to attempt retreat," Boris said. "This does not--"

"We fight," 666 interrupted him, "Nothing can resist soldiers of the DEZA army."

Boris nodded. 666's words had carried the stamp of finality. "Yes, we fight."

Death didn't share her lover's optimism on the positive outcome of the impending conflict with the brains at all.

"We could sure do with that Superzombie freak's help now," she said.

666 snorted. "He is not needed here. We will take care of ourselves."

He nodded at Death. She grunted and moved to his rear, stood back-to-back with him, as did Blueteeth with Boris. An all-around-protection maneuver long ago perfected.

The brains closed in for the attack.

#

The zombies' attack/defense was initially stymied by their fear of brain contamination.

"Use only your guns!" 666 shouted. "Make them keep their distance from us!"

His companions did so. Their brainshit shells did little exterior damage to the brains, penetrating them to explode inside their bodies. They, however, caused the brains sufficient pain to discourage them from closing in on the quartet.

"Eat zombies!!" the brains screamed their choir of frustration, cautious of the gunfire.

"Need to move fast," Death said. "Hunger will soon make them reckless."

"Yes," 666 agreed, he pointed through the brain tunnel at the temple of Necro. "Head for the building."

They moved across the plain, brains on all sides of them.

Then an over-hungry sky-brain broke free from the mass overhead and dropped at them, its craving for undead flesh overriding its sense of caution. Its twenty convoluted mouths spread to rip all their heads off at once.

666 bent back and shot it before it hit them.

Shrilling in pain, the brain slewed away. As it fled, one of its lips snagged on the muzzle of 666's gun, ripping a chunk of meat from its surface.

666 ducked the flying brain meat. It hit Boris in his remaining eye instead.

The zombinator yelped reflexively. Then he wiped his face clean in surprise.

"These brains don't explode us!" he shouted. "*Fight!*"

All three zombinators now dropped their guns and prepared for hand-to-brain combat.

666 released the metal spikes recessed inside his body and flipped out the razor helm inside his head. He now looked like a nail-studded club waiting for a god to wield it.

Blueteeth extended her arms to her sides.

Both her palms split between her third and fourth fingers. The split extended through her wrist and separated her metal radius and ulna up to the elbow, becoming a pair of metal shears.

She clicked her arm-shears and smiled toothily at the brains.

Both of Boris's hands were grapple hooks.

Death stuck her gun into her waistband and nodded.

"Let's do this then," she said. "These fuckers have no idea what's about to hit them."

#

The zombinators' alteration of tactics was their undoing.

Boris swung his right grappler-hand around his head thrice, then slung it at the nearest brain--a huge mass that looked like a skinless testicle from Hell. The grappler struck the brain right at its top, its metal hooks digging deep into the slick surface meat.

Boris yanked his hand down. He was totally unprepared for what happened next.

None of them were.

Like a flimsy curtain, the brain ripped all the way down its front, spewing out a mass of undigested zombies.

There was nothing else inside it, just zombies. Twitching and quivering limbs and a hundred undigested heads that screamed "brains!" piteously.

The brain which Blueteeth had slashed across its front with her shears opened up similarly, revealing that it too was nothing other than a bag full of piecemealed zombies.

A horror unlike any they'd ever experienced before in their endless lives settled on 666, Blueteeth, and Boris.

They looked at the twitching quivering masses of their kin on the ground, then looked at the surrounding brains, realizing each was also packed full of torn-apart zombies.

To be alive as chunks of meat for all eternity--fully conscious but fully impotent-- was the ultimate zombie nightmare. The three zombinators were viewing the timeless definition of zombie Hell.

All their toughness and fight drained from them like urine from an incontinent old woman. With Boris in the lead, they turned and fled towards the Temple of Necro.

All ran in absolute terror, their single thought to reach the safety of the building in the distance.

The brains, themselves initially about to flee upon seeing the effectiveness of the zombies' body-weaponry, now turned and raced after them, gnashing their many jaws in hunger.

Death not being a zombie, the brains could care less about her presence there.

"Shit," Death said, as she watched the brains bear down on the fleeing zombinators. She ran after them.

#

The brains caught the zombinators well before they got anywhere near the temple.

Two of them grabbed Blueteeth between their lowest jaws. While she whimpered in horror, they fucked her, driving their spinal-cord cocks in and out of the gaping holes in her anatomy that she'd picked up from her fall from the helicopter.

They fucked her till they came into her-- black goo that looked like rotten caviar.

Blueteeth immediately expanded and became a brain, spitting out her metal skeleton in chunks through her mouths.

She joined the brains in assaulting her two companions.

Boris was caught by sky-brains. One of them swooped over him and bit off his head with a single chomp. Another clamped its teeth over his shoulders and soared aloft with him, where it engaged in a tug-of-war for his body with six or seven others, the group of them pulling him every which way until he disintegrated between them into chunks of quivering meat.

#

Death caught up with the brains as they were ripping 666 apart.

The head zombinator lay whimpering on the floor, too terrified to defend himself.

A brain had his left leg in a mouth and was tearing it off. Death winced at the sound of his flesh separating.

"Oh no, you don't eat my man," she growled.

She swung into action, touching the brain with her right hand and concentrating on draining force from it. The brain turned black, withered and crumbled to dust.

She reached out to touch another brain, then stopped.

She gaped at her hand in surprise. Its skin was now convoluted, as if it was itself a brain.

*What the fuck is this?* She was so weak suddenly--she felt like she was dying. The ultimate irony. She, death, *dying?*

She reached out and touched another brain that was about to bite 666. It too crumbled to dust, but her weakness became worse.

The brain-like ridging of her skin now extended past her elbow.

She touched another brain and blacked out.

When she came to, she was sitting cross-legged on the floor facing 666, with no memory of when she'd sat down.

She'd never felt so powerless in her life. She sat, rocking left and right like a pendulum each time a brain bumped against her.

"Eat zombie!!" the brains screeched victoriously.

*"No!"* Death gasped, watching in horror as a brain bit off her lover's head.

Two others ripped off his arms.

Another two brains began screwing the rest of 666, sticking their nerve-cocks into his neck cavity and ribcage.

Paralyzed by weakness, Death watched while 666 turned into a spinal cord monster and crawled up to disappear into a crack in a brain's ass end.

She watched the brains a while longer, till she was strong enough to move, then crawled groggily towards the distant Temple of Necro.

# Chapter 7

Superzombie set the headless zombinator down on a table.

He walked over to a lab freezer and got out a plastic tub marked 'Danger: Humancow Brains.'

Carelessly, Superzombie picked out a cold brain. He traced its pale ridges and grooves with his left index finger, savoring the pleasure of not being allergic to it.

He smiled. He replaced the brain in its tub and put the tub back into the freezer.

He then walked over to a wall closet and got out a vial of green liquid and a hypo. One injection and five minutes later, Superzombie was once again Dr. October.

Standing by a mirror, the doctor spent a few minutes plucking withered head-worms from his skull. No point raising anyone's eyebrows.

As always after using his secret serum and its antidote, Dr. October was EXTREMELY hungry. He got eight blood potatoes out of a storage rack and microwaved them, afterwards eating them ravenously.

#

Dr. October was in a quandary. The salvation of zombiehood had so far thrown up nothing but roadblocks on his dogged quest for it.

He'd so far no news of his runaway womancow, his definite answer to the impending exhaustion/extinction of the human meatfields.

She might be dead for all he knew, most likely murdered by those zombie-worshipping religious fanatics, the necros, those philistines unable to appreciate the fact that this universe ran on scientific principles, not the whims of some capricious undead deity.

The re-creation, the fools called this existence. They claimed the god Necro cared more for humans than his own zombie kind and had revealed his truth to them. The vegans, his original chosen, had departed from the faith and needed reconversion.

Dr. October finished his meal of potatoes. He was only part-revived--his muscles ached and his head hurt. He'd eat more later. He'd waited too long before using the antidote this time, a few hours more and he'd have exploded into flame from his head-worm's static electricity buildup.

The doctor's super-serum had begun as a futile attempt at zombie salvation. It worked-- it made the user able to not only touch brains, but even eat meat without ill effects.

Only its cons outweighed its pros.

The primary constituent of the serum was a culture of microscopic mutant worms. Injected into zombie flesh, the minute worms grew instantly into large electrically charged ones (those that Death and the zombinators had seen crawling in and out of Superzombie's skull), which migrated to the user's head.

In addition to providing him immunity to human tissue, the head-worms gave Superzombie the ability to fly, super strength and super vision. And also the power to fire energy bolts from his hands and eyes.

One downside was that the worms never stopped producing power while in him. They had no regulation mechanism whatsoever.

Superzombie couldn't burn all the power off, no matter how much activity he indulged in. His personal voltage kept stacking up.

Dr. October had calculated that spontaneous self-combustion would result if the worms remained in his body for longer than twelve hours.

The antidote killed them as instantly as they grew.

The more serious downside was that each use of his super serum required Dr. October eating sixteen blood potatoes afterwards simply to rejuvenate his body.

Over two week's normal vegan food consumption eaten at one go.

It was the cure that magnified the illness. What use was it being immune to everything, if the immunity itself meant using up the resource powering it at accelerated rates--when the whole idea in the first place was to conserve that resource?

And assuming someone had suggested 'Why not use the serum only at meal times? Why not become super-powered, eat humans, and take the antidote?' Dr. October would have upchucked in disgust at such suggested perversion.

Eat *meat*? Not even the threatened Zombie Stone Age would ever make him sink so low as that.

In his scholastic way Dr. October was as much a fanatic as the necros. All his experiments on meat-toxicity and his Superzombie body had occurred in test tubes.

#

Dr. October sat for a while thinking.

Warden Painfield's death had been reported to him yesterday. He regretted having her killed, but it was unavoidable. If his escaped womancow remained uncaught, there must be no record of her ever having existed.

Her partner 15m currently resided in a locked underground cell, awaiting termination the instant confirmation of 15f's being irretrievable (or her death) reached the doctor.

When it became clear to all that blood potato supplies were running low, the DEZA authorities, nay, vegan zombiehood as a whole, must never know that there had been such a hope and it had come to nothing. It would kill the proud vegan spirit of the breed.

Better they continue their current senseless course of non-conservative farming.

Best to cultivate humans to extinction and go out in a blaze of glory.

Part Six:
God or Someone Dissimilar?

# Chapter 1

Able stepped through the temple door--. He was immediately stopped by two zombie angels.

Both angels were eight feet tall and carried bone swords like Morphia's. Both were skinless, more skeleton than flesh, their internal organs visible through their ribs, their leg and arm bones visible between their muscles.

The wings of both were bony frameworks over which thin flesh stretched like clothes hung out to dry.

Able doubted either zombie angel could fly.

"You're expected, Able Kane," the angel on the left said. "Follow us."

With that both angels turned around and walked off without a backward glance. Able started to follow, when a voice spoke from somewhere both near and far away.

"Take off all your shoes and your clothes, Able Kane. Do not defile my holy place."

The zombie angels had stopped and awaited him.

Able quickly dropped his bag, stripped off, and set off after them.

The temple floor was an expanse of rotting human meat. Like Neck's bed, Able realized.

His feet sank ankle deep into the decayed flesh as he walked, each step rupturing pockets of fetid gas. The bubbles popped on the surface like underwater farts.

A quick look confirmed to him that both angels were walking *over* the meat floor, not *on* it--their stepping soles were inches above its surface.

The walls of the temple were made of zombie flesh, in this case stretched and stitched into rugs. Like he'd been in Neck's presence, Able was overwhelmed.

#

They reached an endless hall.

In the hall a maroon-colored ball floated. The angels disappeared. Able walked forward and saw that the ball was made of meat.

It was about his height, and comprised from every body part imaginable: Brains, livers, hands and feet, breasts--all formed part of its surfaces. Cocks and cunts and anuses packed with shit and suppositories.

There were also incomplete bodies studding it, and bones sticking out of it at odd angles like antennas of ancient spy satellites.

All of the ball's meat was zombie meat. It had that undead unhealthy look to it, which Able, as necros head food technician, could identify in his sleep.

"I am Necro," the ball of undead meat said. "Worship me for I am your god. Reject me at your peril."

Its voice was the voice Able had heard earlier, the one coming from everywhere at once.

Able knelt with his forehead on the meat-floor. It made perfect sense to him that his God looked like this. Didn't the scriptures read that Necro, being unable to make man *in his image*, resurrected the undead as zombies instead?

"You approve of me," Necro said, its voice pleased.

"You are God--the fulfillment of all I am and ever will be. I do not need to approve of you. I worship you."

"Then stand and come and embrace me my child. Come, come."

## Fucking God for Fun and Profit

So Able went forward and embraced the ball of meat. And while he did so, a tongue, snake-long, began licking him all over.

"Eat me," Necro screamed at him with its million voices that came from everywhere at once, including inside Able's flesh.

Able ate God, ripping large chunks of flesh from him: Intestines, liver, a heart, breasts, a penis, even an asshole. The meat was there in front of him, undead and obscene and divine, and he fed and fed until his belly bulged.

At a point during this divine feast he got a hard-on. He felt hands from the ball of meat grip his cock. The hands jerked him off, then inserted him into a tight opening.

He looked down for a moment. His cock had been inserted into an asshole, a putrid hole from which it emerged covered with yellow slime when he pulled it out. The anus was PACKED with purple hemorrhoids and belonged to a pair of cellulite-laden buttocks projecting from Necro's equator. The buttocks ended in thighs from which both legs had been untidily hacked off, blood dripped from their jagged severed ends, smearing Able's thighs in turn.

This was Haeven, as Able had always imagined it in his dreams, as it had been preached (minus this god-fucking bit) by Priest in the Temple of Undeath.

Able laughed and resumed feeding on the ball of meat. While he did so he fucked the buttocks mercilessly.

Then he came forever and ever and ever.

#

Afterwards, he and Necro lay in bed and smoked marijuana. Necro had now become a hairy black foot with foot-long gold toenails. Its truncated ankle was a red-lipsticked mouth.

The zombie angels had brought them some joints and a bottle of wine and left them.

"You are a good fucker, Able Kane," God said. "But you lack finesse."

"I'm only human," Able replied honestly. He took a puff from a joint, placed it between God's lips, so he too could smoke it.

Necro dragged deeply on the joint. Able watched the embers of disintegrating marijuana redden the joint into shortness.

He poured wine between both their lips.

"You are God, my *only* God."

"Not true," Necro said, with some unease. "There is an Elder GOD, He who made the first creation and the devil..." Then Necro snorted petulantly. "Forget him--, I'm in charge here now."

"*He* doesn't count," Able Kane said. "You are the insufficient deity for the worlderness." He licked Necro's hairy toes to calm him.

His reply and actions pleased Necro intensely.

Indeed, everything Able Kane did pleased Necro intensely.

Necro felt *very good*. He considered keeping Able Kane here in Haeven and marrying him, but decided not to. Able Kane was human and impure. He had already caused much disruption to things, would cause yet more if permitted to remain in Haeven.

As had happened to him when he'd met Neck in person, it never once occurred to Able Kane all the while he was with Necro to question his actions. Inquiries about his policies concerning man became irrelevancies.

The fact that Necro was what he was, was sufficient answer for the world's condition.

#

"Return to Earth, Able Kane," Necro-foot said, after their pleasant afterfuck afterglow moment. "You have done damage enough here."

"Humankind is dying," Able said. He stroked the hairy black foot, and rubbed it against his face. "Will you heal the world?"

God giggled. "By your coming here, you have already destroyed it, Able Kane--even now the re-end has come upon the re-creation. But fear not, after everything is over--I will re-

renew my re-creation again. You necros... will be the new zombies. Surely that is only fair?"

Able nodded. "Perfectly, for we are your faithful. We will die in this life to be raised undead in the after-creation to come." He smiled. "So my coming here accomplished something after all?"

God's ankle-mouth smiled. "You accomplished everything I fated and predetermined you to," he said.

#

"Death awaits you outside," Necro said.

"I thought you loved me," Able said.

"It's okay, she's unemployed at the moment--I do all my own killing now." God became a ball of gore again, rose to oversee his re-creation once more.

"Take one of the cockrockets out back. Travel through the distant bull's-eye to home. Just take that Death bitch with you."

Able bowed. "Yes, Lord."

He turned to leave, and Necro called him back.

"Able Kane."

"*Yes, Lord?*"

"Tell my people, the necros, that I will give them a sign that they are my chosen. In their hour of direst need, my sun will come and deliver them. Do not forget this: I will send them my sun to save them."

"Yes, my lord."

The zombie angels returned immediately. They escorted him out of the temple.

# Chapter 2

Outside, Able Kane noted that there was now something very odd going on. Brains and zombies were pouring through the hole in Haeven's floor which Soil had created and fallen through.

He realized they were all falling to earth. The brains and zombies streamed towards and into the hole as relentlessly as if someone was vacuuming them through it from the other side.

This is bad, Able thought, really bad.

He looked up at his giant escorts. "What is going on here?"

The zombie angels smiled dead smiles at him. "Remember our Lord's words to you."

Able remembered Necro's words: 'Even now the re-end has come upon the re-creation.'

Urgency possessed him. He had to get back downstairs already.

#

Able found Death around the temple corner. She was laid out on the temple steps, looking wasted.

"Hey..." he began. Then he stared in horror at the sight of her face--the protuberant eyes, the horrid nose that looked like an erect cock, the knife-wound mouth...

*If looks could kill...* Able suddenly *knew* hers had--times without number.

Death looked groggily up at him. Her arm had lost its brain-texture now and she felt bedraggled, worse than she had since... since being forced into retirement by that ball of fetid meat inside this building.

"Who the fuck are *you*?"

"He's under God's protection," the two zombie angels told her. "Don't you dare fuck with him. Or else..." They turned and vanished back into the temple.

When Able had gotten over the shock of the horribleness of her features, he helped her to her feet. They had to get moving fast.

Death had no idea of his sense of urgency. She attempted to shake his hands off, but was too weak. She swayed like a drunken starlet at an ancient Hollywood party.

Able rushed her along the steps towards the back of the temple where their transport waited. Death didn't appreciate being forced to move. She was mourning 666 and had no time for this crap.

Her knife-wound shark-mouth split into a feral snarl:

"Where the fuck are you taking me? I don't do rape, whatever meatball inside told you."

Able decided he seriously disliked Death. "I'm taking you back down to Earth, where you *don't* belong. Now could you *please* seriously *move your ass*?"

Part Seven:
When the world is running
down, you make the best of
dinosaurs around...

(Or, Welcome to the Zombie Stone Age)

# Chapter 1

## *Soil's return*

Soil fell and fell and crashed directly onto the east wall of her old home Vegfarm 642.

She grunted in discomfort for a moment and stood up. Though she'd fallen from Haeven, she was unharmed.

Her fall had, however, totally demolished the entire wall she'd landed on. It was now rubble interspersed with pulped zombie-guards. Deep troughs marked where her many bone projections had punctured into the ground.

Soil, the humanosauraus, was now larger than Vegfarm 642--and ravenously hungry. Though no longer possessing human intellect, she was nonetheless drawn by one memory.

She headed for the farm cafeteria, stamping fleeing humancows into the ground like ants. They looked like the red 'kill' smears in ancient videogames.

Soil ripped the roof off the cafeteria. She swatted the disbelieving zombie servers aside and scooped out handfuls of roasting corpses and stuffed them into her mouth. All the food in the cafeteria made little difference to Soil's hunger, however, so she began eating the humancows. She scooped them up in bunches and plunged them into her jagged-toothed maw.

This was much better.

The humancows had no protection whatsoever from Soil, neither had the zombies, but she ignored those. Zombies smelled totally wrong to her and made her feel like puking. Only human flesh smelled and tasted right.

When she'd eaten about five hundred humancows (and unwittingly stamped another two hundred more into the farm muck), she felt better. Not totally full, but close.

She also now felt another urge.

She cocked a leg over the farm and sprayed it with a heavy shower of urine, a rain of pee that soaked everyone and everything, inundating the ground and buildings.

Soil finished peeing. She sat on the farm power plant (crumbling it completely into the ground) and masturbated, zipping her cuntbag zipper up and down furiously till she came with a violence that made her inadvertently flail out her other arm, smashing Warden Painfield's erstwhile office to bits.

She felt sated after that. She dozed for a few minutes.

When she awoke she looked around for more humans to eat. There were none. This puzzled her, as did the fact that the farm now thronged with a hundred littler versions of herself.

She shrugged. Now her sexual hunger was assuaged, its physical counterpart had revived. She left the farm--she could smell many other vegfarms all around her, all packed full with juicy humancows to eat.

Oh, oh, how hungry she suddenly was.

#

The effect of Soil urinating on the humancows of Vegfarm 642 (and on each farm she subsequently visited and destroyed) was immediate: They all transformed into humanosaurs like herself. Growing larger by the moment, the male and female lizards each bounded out into the worlderness looking for human flesh to feed on.

Their targets were the human settlements in the wilderness.

They stormed these like locusts, decimating the hapless human populations even more completely than the necros had.

The humanosauruses didn't waste food. After eating what human portions they needed for immediate satisfaction of their hunger, the female humanosaurs stored all leftover meat in their (now humongous) cuntbags for easy retrieval and later consumption.

# Chapter 2

## *(Able) Kane's fall from grace*

The cockship parked out back was a replica of those Able had passed while ascending the side of the lemon tree.

The ancient NASA space shuttle lay on an inclined earthen rise, pointing at an archer's target.

The target was a flayed Negro woman's skin, tacked to the side of a house. The skin from the rear of her body was folded out sideways so that it extended either side of her.

She was laid out spread eagled. Her face had been repositioned below her breasts, in the middle of her belly, with her mouth stretched out into a wide 'O'.

"That's the bulls-eye?"

Death had now begun re-collecting her addled wits from the ether around her. "Don't even bother *trying* to reason this out," she said. "She gives us head, and we're out of here yesterday."

Able nodded. He swung open the cockrocket's testes door and they entered.

The rocket interior had forward-facing seats set on either side of a central aisle. The seats were occupied by a large number of skeletons. Most of the skeletons belonged to children.

"Commercial flights," Death explained to her perplexed companion. "I think this was a school flight to the Moon, back when Earth still had one."

Able concealed his deep ignorance of history with a nod.

They tramped layers of bones through to the cockpit.

"Let *me* fly this," Death said, clearing the pilot's bones from the seat on their left.

"Let me," Able insisted in return. "You don't look in any condition to fly anything."

"You don't know how anyway," Death said triumphantly, sitting in the shuttle's control seat. "Now which knob does what again?"

Able agreed she was right. He cleared the co-pilot's bones away and sat down beside her.

To quench his rising fears that she was going to crash them, he began reading aloud from his copy of The Book of Undeath; not looking up from its pages till she had the rocket in the air and heading toward the black woman-skin tacked to the building wall.

She came at them fast, her mouth expanding like a purple-lipped black hole.

Able asked the obvious question. "Are we getting smaller, or is she getting bigger?"

Death shrugged. "What do you care? Long as we make it through her face I'm fine with either."

The cockrocket slid through the woman's stretched lips and blew out into the sky below Haeven. Looking out through the cockpit windows as Death stabilized the vehicle, Able saw they'd come out close to the opening through which the zombies and brains were falling.

Neither brains nor zombies fell directly to earth. Instead, they separated into types and spread sideways beneath the roof of the worlderness, as they went collecting into brain and zombie clouds that spread and spread farther and farther afield.

"It will rain zombies someday soon," Able said.

Death shrugged. "Rain brains too. So what else is new?" She looked at him, frowning. "Look, you wanna go home or what?"

Able took another look at the odd clusters spreading out through the sky. 'Or what?' might actually be better.

Then he remembered he had Necro's message about the sun to deliver to his people. "Do not forget this," God had said.

Able was a very conscientious believer.

"Take me home, girl," he said wearily.

Death smiled nastily at him. "*Girl,* eh? Yeah, I think you're fucking cute too."

She dropped the shuttle beneath the brain and zombie clouds and pointed it towards the necros kingdom.

#

In the temple of Necro on Death Raft 4, Neck--God in Flesh and Priest of the necros--was concluding the rites of evening worship.

The hermaphrodite xombina stood on an altar, naked except for her Priest's robe of zombie faces. Before her on a lectern lay open a copy of the Book of Undeath, from which she read the closing litany.

"We his chosen people worship Necro because his will is ultimate," she intoned. "He is the imperfection imperfecting our imperfections, just as he imperfects this imperfect world."

"We are impure, unworthy of all his blessings," the congregation intoned solemnly back at her. "Oh Necro you are great, in your mercy you give us zombie to eat. You give zombie to us also for clothes and houses, and for purging our carnal desires."

"Eat wear build fuck zombie!"

"Eat wear build fuck zombie!"

"Necro is all in all!"

"All in all is Necro!"

"Necro is all in all!"

"Eat wear build fu--"

The NASA shuttle cockrocket crashed through the temple roof, killing a quarter of the assembled worshippers.

It had run out of brainshit fuel two minutes ago, and Death had been fighting to control it ever since.

The dust cleared. The screams of the perplexed subsided. The testicle door swung open and Death and Able Kane stepped out.

"You would not believe where I've just been," Able said, wiping fear-sweat off his brow.

The congregation just gaped at him.

Able realized then that he'd forgotten his clothes in Haeven, such had been the glory of Necro. All he'd *somehow* managed to take from the temple was his copy of the Book of Undeath. He'd even forgotten his precious cure.

He covered his privates with his hands.

Neck said nothing. She stood on the altar, watching, glorious in her robe of watching faces.

She was nervous. She pulled out a handful of maggots from her belly and ate them, chewing rhythmically to calm the sense of anticipation threatening to overwhelm her. A white sludge of masticated larva spilled out of her face through the hole that was her left cheek.

Part of Neck's problem was her remembrance of Able's recent blasphemy. The xombina was, however, politically astute enough to realize that to rule successfully, one could not nurse grudges where issues of power were concerned.

She watched, trying to decide the right course of action.

"Should we arrest him?" The priests on the floor below her debated amongst themselves.

"We should listen to him first," one said.

"We must kill the blasphemer," another said. "Purge his evil from among us. He is Hereticos incarnate. See, he arrives in a *cockrocket*, the vehicle of Hellfire."

The others agreed with this last.

Three holy assassins charged at Able, knives raised.

Death stepped between him and them. She touched two. Both blackened and disintegrated into charred hulks that crumpled into ash. The third shrank back.

"I can do this all day long," she said simply.

"Wait," Neck said, deciding to play along with what was happening. Able's ugly companion could prove a major nuisance otherwise.

She stepped down from the altar. "He has something to say." She beckoned Able forward. "My child, what message do you bring?"

"My Lord in Flesh," Able said respectfully with a deep bow. "My female companion here is Death. We come from Haeven."

At the word 'Haeven' there was a loud explosion of murmuring in the congregation; whispers of 'blasphemy.'

Neck swallowed her mouthful of maggots. "Silence!" she shouted. "Go on, my child," she told Able.

Able nodded. "It's true, my Lord Neck. With my own eyes, I saw our lord Necro, and he had this to say to all necros..."

# Chapter 3

The vegan DEZA authorities could only watch the destruction of their food supply in horror.

The vegan army flew out in choppers. Their brainshit weaponry was useless against the armored skin of the humanosaurs, even bombs merely blew craters around the beasts and left them unharmed.

In addition, their chopper cleavers dented on the human-dinosaur's massive body teeth.

With the humanosaurs increasing both in numbers and size all the time, the zombies thought they had it bad. Only, it got much worse.

Around this time, the first sightings of raining zombies and brains were reported, dispersed out all over DEZA and the worlderness.

# Chapter 4

Dr. October reacted immediately as the news reached him of the vegan crisis. He rushed to his wall cabinet and got out his superserum and injected himself.

Five minutes later, as his secret identity, Superzombie, he was flying towards the monstrous Soil at the speed of sound.

#

A bolt of gray lightning, Superzombie streaked across the countryside. He was shocked by the extent of damage to the vegfarms. Farm after farm after farm lay in ruins, with humancows turned humanosaurs clambering over the ruined walls that had once imprisoned them.

This was a national crisis of the highest order.

Superzombie didn't stop to tackle any of the littler humanosaurs. His focus was the monster tooth-covered dinosaur up ahead, now standing rear-leg cocked over trampled buildings, and letting rip with a stream of yellow pee that stank up to where he was, two miles away.

Superzombie headed for Soil.

#

Reaching her, it was with horror he read off the huge ID on the monster's forehead. 15f. *Oh, no.* This was *his* fault?

There would be enough time for self-recrimination later, he decided. Now was time to fight, not think.

They engaged in combat, a fight lasting less than a minute. Despite Superzombie's great powers, he was no match for the womanosaurus. Soil swatted him away like a fly, so hard that he was driven right through the crust of the Earth.

The fall knocked superzombie out cold. He lay unconscious, deep below the Earth's surface, his head-worms sizzling, while above him, creation warped on its hinges.

# Chapter 5

## *A narrative:*
## *Breakdown of the undead man.*

*A paraphrase of Book IV of the First Chronicles of the Undead:  Chapters V to IX.*

The zombies rained like rain, falling gently and endlessly.  Each landed on a cushion of air, then picked themselves up and staggered off, moaning "brains!"

The rained brains didn't remain on the ground after impact.  Each bounced aloft again immediately, with a zombie (or three or four) trapped between its many jaws, and floated away to feed on them, descending to catch more zombies once it was hungry again.

What had ordained in Haeven now ordained on Earth also, with brains killing and eating undead both sides and center.

Only now the brains had the vegan zombies and xombinas of the DEZA kingdom to feed on also.

#

It took a while for the vegans to realize they were under attack.  When they did, they found themselves outnumbered on two fronts.

There was seemingly no end to the raining brains, just as there seemed no end to the number of humanosauruses.

The human dinosaurs increased exponentially.

Like Soil, they were uninterested in zombie meat. Their interest in attacking the thousands of vegfarms was because in their transformed state, they smelled other, non-dinosaur humancows as meat good to eat.

Contact, however minimal, with humanosaur urine, spread Able Kane's 'cure' exponentially through the humancow populations.

Worse even than the new species' ravenousness, was the incidental/collateral damage they caused.

For the first time, vegan scientists and military tacticians discovered that, rather than their situation of vegfarms being best from both logistical and defensive standpoints, the locations of the multitude of brainshit power plants that fuelled the DEZA kingdom was a total disadvantage.

The humanosaurs blunderingly destroyed eighty percent of the vegfarm power plants in the first six hours of their transformed existence. Fifteen of the remaining twenty percent were smoking ruins of brick ash before the week ran out.

In almost every case, the humancows' motivation for destroying the power plants was reaching the caches of brains each held, so they could eat them. In the few exceptions, they simply trampled through them on their way to the slaughterhouses, where there were fresh juicy corpses for food.

Explosion after explosion rocked the Neo La skyline, each one concurrent with an area of the DEZA kingdom losing its power supply.

It was the meltdown of zombie civilization as no one had ever envisaged it. The new Stone Age had come early.

#

If the zombies mounted resistance, however futile against the humanosaurs, they stood no chance at all against the brains.

It wasn't so much that the brains were invulnerable, but that the defenders dreaded seeing what they contained. Brains after brains were exploded by the vegan army into nothing but piles of chunked zombies.

The result was a repeat of what had occurred with 666 and his zombinator posse. Unreasoning horror and dread seized the soldiers, causing them to flee their defense posts, vehicles and aircraft. The soldiers' flight generally ended with their being caught by the brains and either eaten or gangbanged into obscene new shapes.

#

Finally, with blood potato stocks at practically zero, most zombies reverted for good back to 'old time Hollywood mode'--mindless creatures with only one thing on their minds-- brains. They left the cities in droves, shambling out into the worlderness, moaning their head-content litany.

And being hunted and eaten by brains.

And yet more and more brains and zombies poured through the hole in the worlderness's ceiling/Haeven's floor.

#

The DEZA themselves escaped the meltdown. Against the event of a necros siege, the vegan king and his court had secretly hoarded blood potato stocks of close to inestimable magnitude. Armed with enough food to keep a small group going for decades (a century even, one scientist estimated), they retreated to a hollowed-out retreat in a mountainside, to wait out the zombie apocalypse, and maybe birth a fresh zombie renaissance at its ending.

Given that length of time, anything was possible.

# Chapter 6

## *Yeeb and Nola*

### I.

Yeeb glanced back over his shoulder at the packs of wired brainshit explosive stacked ceiling-high in the rear of his hoverbus.

He grimaced. *Time to feed those necros assholes some of their own violent excrement for a change,* he thought. *I'm sure they'll enjoy its bitter taste.*

Yeeb the scavenger was the sole survivor of the massacre of Dutchi by the necros a week before. He'd returned from a junk collecting trip to find everyone--even little babies--butchered, their brains removed to fuel the necros feud with the vegans.

Worst of all, Nola was missing. Yeeb had searched the smoking ruins of Dutchi for two days, unable to find her corpse.

Yeeb was handsome, tall, and muscular, with a body heavily scarred by worlderness living.

At the moment he had a long pale tendril of meat growing out of the bottom of his left ear.

Yeeb believed in action rather than thought. Words meant little; achieved even less. Violence, however, shaped both now and the future.

He considered both the vegan zombie monsters and necros fanatics as empirical proof of his theory.

Neither side clearly thought much. The vegans were killing everyone for food and energy, and the necros were killing everyone left for bigotry and weaponry.

But they ran the worlderness.

Yeeb was tired of endlessly fearing both necros and zombies, sick of endlessly anticipating waking one morning to find himself trapped by either group of shithead assholes. Or between them.

Ironically, the vegans and zombies had provided Yeeb with a profession. Suppressing his fear of both parties, he'd travelled the worlderness in their wake, looting the destruction left by their raids for things to use or sell.

Nola usually travelled with him, but this time, she'd stayed home to nurse her sick mother. *And what was the fucking result? Fucking abduction!*

For years now, Nola Fali had been the only beautiful thing in Yeeb's life. He intended getting her back.

#

Yeeb's vehicle was a hoverbus salvaged/cobbled-together from necros and zombie wreckage. Yeeb's gift for messing with scrap technology had led him into his current profession.

Since deciding to rescue Nola, he'd been busy. In increasing desperation, he'd scoured the worlderness looking for explosives--a shitload of them.

His task was made harder by his need to dodge the monster tooth-covered dinosaurs. He also steered well clear of areas with high overhead brain concentrations.

Three days ago he'd reached a vegan settlement pillaged by the necros, full of brain-exploded moving pieces of the undead. By climbing down into the settlement power plant's fuel tanks and patiently scraping their walls clean with a bone knife, Yeeb had salvaged six buckets of brainshit explosive.

Adding that amount to Dutchi's own brainshit stocks, none of which the necros had found, Yeeb now had sufficient explosive to almost fill the rear of the hoverbus.

A day spent wiring his vehicle with the explosives and vegan primers had effectively turned Yeeb's hoverbus into a brainshit bomb.

Point it at the target, one remote-controlled click and... Boom!

He'd just enough space left in the rear of the hoverbus afterwards to stash a hoverbike, water and two crates of blood potatoes.

#

Yeeb had found the crates of blood potatoes in the zombie village. One currently rested beside him on the bus's passenger seat.

He reached across and picked a potato from it.

The blood potato wriggled like a worm in his hand. He was accustomed to that now. It was warm. It felt like he was holding a sponge rat. He almost could imagine a heartbeat transmitting vibrations into his palm and fingers. He shook his head at the thought; it *wasn't* alive, thank God.

But it sure looked like it was: Its pseudoface, its unblinking black pseudoeyes, its myriad of nerve tendrils. And the way it kept pulsing like a severed heart.

"I hate these things," Yeeb had told Nola six months ago, "they're creepy as zombies."

"That's why they go so well together," she'd replied. "They're like vegan babies. And they're so *cute*."

She'd taken the blood potato from him and cooed at it: "How's my little baby veggie today?"

Yeeb had snapped at her. "Stop doing that!"

Now, his mind snapped back to the present and the worlderness ahead. He yelped, dropped the blood potato, grabbed the wheel with both hands, and swerved the bus hard right.

His reflexes were fast enough now to avoid crashing into the humanosaur charging across the barren wastes ahead.

Yeeb stopped the hoverbus and sat back sweating, staring after the human-dinosaur.

"Shit!"

The humanosaur was chasing a vegan chopper dangling a net-full of human captives. The chopper was already damaged, both its left cleaver hands ripped off its fuselage. It flew lopsided.

The humanosaur was wounded--its trunk bore deep slashes, and blood poured from a large hole on its left shoulder. Clearly, the vegan troops had been fending it off for a while.

Still it chased after the fleeing helicopter, hungry for the vegans' human captives, all loudly screaming at the zombie pilots to fly the damn machine *fucking faster*.

"*Lucky for me,*" Yeeb thought, after his heart stopped pounding.

He dismissed the fleeing zombies and their unfortunate human cargo from his mind. The incident was simply a sign of these horrible times when action spoke larger than thought.

Once sure he was in no danger of the humanosaur returning his way, he retrieved his dropped blood potato from the hoverbus floor, and bit deeply into it.

"Lunchtime," he murmured.

Since finding the crate of blood potatoes, Yeeb had become addicted to them. From tentatively taking a bite of one to find out what it tasted like, he'd now become consumed by the compulsion to eat them.

Nola had warned him off previous experiments, but she wasn't here now. And Yeeb had found that eating the potatoes immediately boosted his energy levels. He was able to think sharper and move faster.

Just like avoiding the humanosaur just now.

264 | Vegan Zombie Apocalypse

The downside to eating the blood potatoes was that he'd begun growing tendrils on his body.

The meaty filaments sprouted in ones or twos all over him. They grew in mere minutes and pulling them out hurt like shit.

He wrapped his fingers now around the pale white feeler of meat dangling from the lowest lobe of his left ear and yanked on it. He'd discovered that did the trick--one sharp tug and the tendril came free in his hand. It left a small crater like a smallpox scar in his earlobe, and pain like a transposed headache. Yeeb tossed the tendril out of the window and took another bite of blood potato.

He couldn't stop eating the potatoes now. He needed the energy they provided. But once he'd freed Nola, he'd kick them for good.

#

Yeeb's plan was simple: Infiltrate the death raft that had taken Nola and rescue her.

It was a suicidal idea at the best of times. These, however, weren't the best of times.

With zombies and brains raining non-stop, and giant tooth-covered human-lizards running amok everywhere, there was so much uncertainty everywhere now that... even the clearly impossible seemed even more clearly possible. How long this present atmosphere of uncertainty would last was anyone's guess, but Yeeb intended taking full advantage of the necros' currently divided attentions.

He had a reason for attacking *today*. This was the seventh day since the necros assholes had raped and pillaged Dutchi. Meaning today they would initiate their surviving captives as necros shitheads like themselves.

Yeeb had no idea which death raft had destroyed Dutchi and taken Nola, but he was certain they'd be at Salt Lake. For some reason the necros always inducted new members at Salt Lake in the Utah plains.

There'd be no guards. Why should there be? No non-necros had ever dared go there.

Until fucking now, that is.

Everyone on a death raft took part in the Copro ceremony. They'd all be in the temple. He'd have no better time to rescue Nola. And then strike back at them. Blow the fuckers to kingdom gone with his bus-bomb.

Yeeb *knew* Nola was still alive. She was beautiful and the necros never killed beautiful women. *Fucking pervs*.

## II.

"You necros are *total* perverts," Death told Able Kane. "You know that, don't you?"

They were seated in the temple hut along with the entire necros population of Death Raft 4, awaiting the commencement of the Copro ceremony.

(The temple hut had now been expanded outward on the side opposite where Death had crashed landed the cockrocket. The rocket remained where it had landed, visible proof to all the faithful of Necro's divine intervention.

The dead necros had been left to decay to skeletons beneath it.

Necros engineers had already installed additional antigrav engines under the temple floor at that point to stabilize the death raft.)

Able ignored Death. It wasn't her ugliness--he'd been with unpretty women before-- he just didn't think Death was something/someone anyone should be on chatty terms with.

He couldn't ignore her utterly fantastic body, however; the most incredible female body he'd ever seen. She was built like... like... Like a goddess should be.

From toe tips to neck, Death was a total sexual fairy tale, a walking wet dream. That ass...

Those novices who'd survived pain purification were emerging now from the temple offices: Eighteen of them, all naked, all shaven bald for the ceremony. They were led by Mamasi, an immensely fat black woman, also naked. After the novices came Neck in her robe of faces. She-Kill, the new necros army head, followed, accompanied by armed guards.

"I said you necros are fucking perverts," Death repeated. "And stop pretending I'm not talking to you."

Able gave up on ignoring her. "It's tradition, even if you're born necros you must go through it as a rite of passage."

Able hadn't been too surprised to find, on returning home, both Priest and Morphia dead and Neck in political ascent. He still felt the horrible urge to fall and worship every time he saw the xombina. He agreed God was the perfect candidate to be his own priest.

But now the euphoria of visiting Haeven had worn off, he was having trouble adjusting to the fact that most necros now regarded him as a prophet.

He'd brought them the Word of God after all.

The priests of Necro absolutely hated his new influence, the way everyone constantly looked to him for confirmation of doctrine. Able had met Necro in person, they reasoned; therefore Able *knew for sure*.

Able had omitted all mention of screwing God from his account of his travels.

On Death's advice, he'd also remained aloof from all religious discussion, keeping his mouth shut and looking solemn and wise. He suspected the only reason Neck hadn't yet invited him to spend the night in the holy hut with her, was because Death remained eternally by his side like they were conjoined twins.

Despite his reservations about her, Able was very grateful to Death for staying. Without her around he doubted it would be long before his former assistant Beni mobilized disgruntled priests to assassinate him.

He also didn't like the black looks the new military head kept giving him.

When the hell had *he* ever offended *her*? Or was it some carryover something that *Morphia* had done? Or was she just pissed he wasn't chatting her up like she expected, seeing as she was Morphia's successor?

She-Kill's partner had died in the zombie attack on the morning he'd fled from Priest. So she *was* available. But couldn't she just chat up Beni, who was also single?

He realized Death was saying something.

"Huh?"

"Stop ignoring me."

"I'm not. I was just thinking how nice it is, you deciding to stay here for awhile."

She smiled her shark's smile.

Able realized she'd misinterpreted his comment. "What were you saying earlier?"

"I was asking you how this ceremony came about."

"No idea. Honest."

The novices walked past them for their inspection. All were bloodied and bruised from their purification torture.

One of the novices held Able's attention. A slim beauty he'd noticed before. Nola Fali. She reminded him of Morphia--strong, athletic and with a calm self-possessed look about her.

He smiled at Nola wistfully. She affected not to notice his gaze.

"Pay attention to *me*, will you?" Death said, in what Able realized was a warningly jealous tone of voice.

Death had kept him alive so far and had been good to him. There was no point angering her because of another woman. Able pulled his eyes away from the gorgeous Nola and gave Death his full attention.

# III.

Yeeb drove past a crashed brain, its undead stuffing spread across the worlderness like a vomited breakfast. Half the brain was still alive. Its rear surface thronged with spinal-cord creatures that penetrated and exited its crevices like sexually frustrated lovers.

Yeeb yanked off two meat tendrils that suddenly spurted out of his nose and drove on over the spew-trail of twitching zombie meat.

#

Thirty miles from Salt Lake and Death Raft 4, Yeeb came on the remains of the chopper the humanosaur had been chasing earlier.

The helicopter was now damaged well beyond repair, crumpled like a can. Both its propellers were mangled, their blades bent like geriatric fingers. Only one of its arms was still attached to it, and that one was cleaver-less.

*Serves you veggie assholes right,* Yeeb thought savagely.

Of the net-full of kidnapped humans the zombies had been ferrying, there was no sight-- human dino-food for sure now.

Broken zombie limbs poked from the shattered cockpit, jerking spasmodically.

A lone xombina soldier was pulling herself from the wreckage.

Yeeb drove straight at her, ramming her against the side of the chopper. Reversing the hoverbus, he noted with satisfaction that she fell to the ground in three separate pieces.

*Fuck you, veggie bitch.*

Despite his urgency, his scavenger's instincts overrode his caution. If his luck was in, this aircraft could have a still-functioning brain-box. After a cursory glance to ensure the humanosaur wasn't anywhere close, he left the hoverbus for a quick search of any loot-worthy items.

Screwdrivers in hand, he removed the chopper's side panel.

His head and shoulders stuck inside the machine, Yeeb quickly peeled away the layers of shielding over the chopper's guidance system. He punctuated his exertions with bites of blood potato.

On removing the final plastic cover, he sighed in disappointment. A thick metal girder had broken loose from the chopper's undercarriage and speared through the brain box from beneath, reducing it to little more than a mess of gray meat and multicolored wires.

*Shit,* Yeeb thought, *I was this fucking close.*

He realized he was no longer alone. Disbelieving that he'd not noticed its approach; Yeeb extracted himself from the chopper fuselage and stared up at the humanosaurus watching him intently over the wrecked helicopter.

*I'm so, so, so fucked.*

The manosaur dwarfed the chopper. The human-dinosaur's ID was 15m.

His mouth and teeth were soaked with blood. In addition, a human arm dangled forgotten in his left upper jaw, wedged between two teeth. The arm swung like it was waving at Yeeb when the humanosaurus sniffed the air in his direction.

Yeeb was rooted to the spot with fear.

Then the manosaur totally lost interest in Yeeb. The intent look in his yellow eyes faded, and next thing, he turned and walked off, stomping the chopper's tail into the ground as he headed off across the worlderness, back the way Yeeb had come from.

Yeeb watched the monster tramp off into the distance in puzzlement. He understood that he was still alive, but not why. Then a fierce itching in his groin forced him to yank down his trousers.

He stared in disbelief at the meaty tendrils growing out of his cock. *What the...* This potato-eating shit had become more trouble than it was worth.

Then he *understood*: The fucking potatoes were altering his body. He hadn't smelled *right* to the manosaur.

Yeeb immediately revised his opinion on his blood potato consumption. Steeling himself against the pain to follow, he wrapped his fingers around one of the meat tendrils growing out of his penis and yanked it out.

Yeoooooowww! *Fucking hell that hurt.*

He had to pull out ten tendrils. Afterwards, feeling like he'd have done better to have simply cut off his cock, he staggered back to the hoverbus, and resumed speeding toward Salt Lake. After a moment's cautionary reflection, he picked a blood potato out of the crate by his side and bit into it.

Just in case there were any more humanosaurs along his route.

#

Yeeb parked the hoverbus a mile from the temporarily stationary Death Raft 4, behind a low hill.

From the hilltop he gaped, surprised at the death raft opposite him. He knew at once this was no ordinary hovervillage he was viewing, because it was solitary.

Only one necros raft roamed solitary: Death Raft 4, capital of the necros nation.

A thrill filled Yeeb. He'd not only rescue Nola and have revenge for his dead kin, but he'd throw the zombie-fucking necros vulture culture into total disarray--jumpstart the human revolution against the assholes.

The current insanity of raining brains and zombies insisted it was possible.

*Decapitate a body and it will die.*

The necros never protected Death Raft 4 because of some bullshit about Necro never allowing anything evil to happen to it.

*Bullshit asshole superstition. I'll see how you explain my exploding it to bits with a hoverbus-sized brainshit bomb.*

But first he had to rescue Nola.

Yeeb descended back down to the hoverbus, and dressed himself in woven-zombie clothing scavenged from dead necros bodies.

He waited till the sun had almost disappeared over the horizon before starting out over the Utah plains on foot. He timed his progress to arrive at the necros stronghold with nightfall, when the Copro ceremony would be well underway.

He left the hoverbike in the hoverbus. There was the slightest chance someone might notice the fading daylight reflecting off it if he rode it over.

Yeeb planned to get in, get Nola, get out, blow the necros sky-high, and get lost (along with Nola) on the hoverbike.

*This is so easy it's ridiculous,* he thought as he walked.

## IV.

The necros gathering was silent. In their middle, Mamasi now lay on her back on the temple meat bed. Floating on rotting human meat, the fat black woman shut her legs, clenched her ass cheeks, and let out a loud liquid fart.

The congregation sighed at the sound. Able visualized the divine feces popping from her asshole, creamy like a mother's regenerative milk.

Mamasi spread her legs wide again like wings, so the congregation could all see the light-brown shit now thickly coating her ass cheeks like a birthmark.

Mamasi was a shit expert. She could defecate in controlled degrees, a talent required for this ceremony.

The potential necros lined up in single file facing her cunt.

Neck spoke. "Before now you were all less than shit. No necros would permit you to lick the feces from our anuses. You would dirty our holes with your heresy. But now..." Her eyes played over the assembled novices. "...I have a question for you: Do you believe in Necro the imperfect, the God of this re-creation?"

"We do."

"Then lick the shit from Mamasi's ass to show that you are indeed qualified to do so."

The first novice in line, a heavily muscled man named Beeli, climbed onto the meat bed. He knelt between Mamasi's immense thighs and after a moment's hesitation, began licking her humongous ass clean of excrement.

He lapped at it quickly, doing his best to get it over with as fast as possible, working to let the shit rest on his tongue for the briefest of moments before swallowing it.

Neck, She-Kill and the guards watched him intently. Beeli's face showed his revulsion, but he mastered the almost overwhelming urge to throw up the vileness he was being forced to ingest. He finally got it all down inside his furiously revolting belly.

He climbed down off the meat bed and waited expectantly, realizing with surprise that he felt oddly exalted rather than degraded.

Neck smiled at him. She nodded. "You are a true necros, Beeli."

Beeli smiled back and walked over to where the tattooist would inscribe his scalp with its first necros runes.

Mamasi shut her legs again and reopened them with her ass once again smeared with foulness. The next candidate, a gorgeously beautiful pregnant black woman, knelt between her legs and began eating her shit.

## V.

Dressed in his necros garb, Yeeb infiltrated both Death Raft 4 and the temple.

Before clambering aboard the death raft, he took some time to de-tendril himself again. He restricted himself to those on his arms, face and head. Three had grown out of his chin. His back and legs also bristled with them, but thankfully none had sprouted on his cock again.

He was armed with a zombie-bone sword. His pockets were stuffed with blood potatoes, in case he needed to energize up fast.

He pulled himself up over the raft's rim. *I'm coming for you Nola baby. And then we'll blow these fuckhead zombie worshippers to kingdom gone. Assholes.*

No one in the temple looked at him twice. Everyone's attention was riveted on the nobodies becoming necros. Yeeb looked over to the meat bed. His heart skipped a beat when he saw Nola in line there.

#

The Copro ceremony went smoothly until the sixth candidate. Try as he might, Barri Mey could not swallow the cream of excrement in his mouth. It tasted like... *shit*. Just when he thought he'd gotten it down, his throat betrayed him and he expelled it in a stream of vomit that coated Mamasi's bulk like liquid clothing.

Dizzy, Barri staggered off the bed, not even hearing Neck screaming at him in a blood-curdling voice. "You, Barri, are a disgrace to Necro's re-creation! Die!!!"

On those words, the guards butchered Barri where he stood. Then they piled the chunks of his corpse atop Mamasi's body in the meat bed.

Mamasi re-creamed her ass with excrement and the ceremony continued.

"I have to say I like the killing part of necros culture better," Death said. "This endless shit-licking is boring."

"It's a once-in-a-lifetime experience," Able countered. "After now, all heretics are under their excrement as well."

"Fantastic logic, you eat shit to show you're not too impure to eat shit."

Her mockery was lost on Able. "Exactly."

## VI.

Nola Fali climbed onto the meat bed and stuck out her tongue.

*Fuck,* she thought. *If only I'd left mum with Uncle Yakubi and gone with Yeeb on that last trip. But no, I had to play the fucking loving daughter.*

With each lick and swallow of Mamasi's shit, Nola was certain she'd throw up--her stomach was empty, and the taste excruciatingly horrible. The smell was worse, it was mingled with the stink of Mamasi's cunt, which yawned open by Nola's nose like it was begging to be fisted. The Negress's cunt hair was crusted with red and brown smears. The tails of *three* sponge-rats hung out of her cunt. The rat's blood-soaked rumps twitched like they were praying to the goddess of cunts for mercy.

Nola doubted Mamasi ever douched--if she did, maybe she washed with feces.

Nola licked, she swallowed; shit dribbled down her throat like a slug, like a cock she'd accidentally bitten off, like a disease rushing to infect her.

She licked again.

She came suddenly to the exalted realization that God had put shit in asses for a reason--to keep it as far away from one's mouth as possible.

She steeled herself. She wasn't losing her head like those before her. If she needed to degrade herself to survive--so be it.

(Nola had rehearsed for this horrid moment twice during her incarceration here, tasting and eating her excrement when she defecated so she knew what to expect. She wasn't cracking up now. *Fuck no.*)

Re-motivated by her desire to stay alive, Nola began licking the black anus and buttocks facing her furiously, swiping her tongue back and forth like this shit was the most delicious thing she'd ever eaten.

She swallowed, stuck out her tongue again, swallowed again, stuck out her tongue... She imagined that she was eating grilled zombie liver.

She got it all down.

About to regain her feet, she saw with shock that Mamasi's asshole was actually an eye. The anus-eye blinked at her, then pumped out a camouflage of shit to conceal its true nature again.

Nola felt it then--a churning in her guts that became, not the puke she dreaded, but a calm exalted feeling. She suddenly understood that Necro, God the Imperfect, was well pleased with her.

She licked the residual fecal cream from her lips and saw the xombina goddess Neck was smiling at her.

She'd fucking survived.

#

Yeeb felt like vomiting as he watched Nola swallow the excrement from the fat black bitch's ass. That beautiful mouth he'd kissed? They would all die for this, every single damn one of them.

He watched Nola lick the fat bitch's asshole clean, lick her own lips clean, then stand to receive Neck's blessing. He cursed under his breath as Neck pronounced her a true necros.

Nola now looked out over the crowd and saw Yeeb. Their eyes locked. She quickly hid her shock at his presence and smiled and waved to the crowd.

Yeeb controlled his anger. It was all he could do to keep from rushing at the rotting herm xombina and decapitating her--decapitating all of them.

Suicide, however, wasn't the plan. Rescue was.

A tendril sprouted from his elbow. Quick as a flash he yanked it out and trod on it.

#

Alone of all those in the room, Death noted the exchange of glances between Yeeb and Nola. She also noted the grim frown on his face, alone among all the ecstatic necros surrounding him.

She frowned in turn. Something was very wrong here. A necros man interested in Nola would be pleased she had passed her initiation safely, not be angry about it.

## VII.

After another six candidates, the shit-licking part of the ceremony ended, to loud applause from the assembled. Mamasi was now invisible beneath chunks of body parts of the failed candidates.

"It's always the same ratio," Able told Death. "One third of novices always fail the initiation."

Death laughed. "Guess they don't like Mamasi's ass. Tastes differ you know--they might prefer fat-white-girl shit."

Mamasi rolled the corpse chunks off of herself. She wiped her ass-crack clean with a severed foot and sat on edge of the meat bed, acknowledging the cheers of the congregation with weak flutters of her hand.

"I've never seen anyone look that drained after taking a crap before," Death told Able. "Even a really hard and painful one."

"She wasn't merely shitting. Necro was passing himself out of her."

"You're saying God is shit?"

Able ignored her sarcasm. "Our excrement is one of his many manifestations. Before we eat him, he is zombies. Inside us, he is digested. Out of us, he is shit."

"Ah yeah, zombies; I'd forgotten that part."

#

"It is now time for the dividing," Neck said.

Those candidates who'd so far received their tattoos, Nola inclusive, lined up again, facing her.

"You are now necros like us. One thing remains to make you truly part of our tribe: You must all take lovers. Or rather, they must take you, since you know no one yet well enough to choose for yourselves. Understand this is not a permanent pairing. You may end the union later and be with whoever else you will. But tonight and for the next month, you must sleep in this single necros's bed, in this necros's arms."

The new necros nodded.

"Good," Neck said. "We will begin." She looked around the congregation. "These need lovers. Who will choose first?"

Beni immediately stepped forward and pointed at Nola. "I would like her."

Able winced. Beni had already taken his job and now...

Neck peered intently at Nola.

"Our head of food production chooses you. You are fortunate. Do you agree to go with him?"

Nola's face was expressionless. Beni's importance was by no means lost on her. "As my lord God-in-Flesh wishes."

"Well said. But you too are necros now, you have a choice. You are beautiful. If you refuse him, there are other men who will choose you."

Nola immediately glanced over at *the prophet*, Able Kane. Able caught the look, her eyes' flicker of invitation. *She wants me to choose her*, he realized. He could; he ranked over Beni in the people's eyes.

Yes, Nola would be his. He made a move to get up and stake a claim to her.

Death laid a hand on Able's arm, preventing him from standing.

"Don't," she said firmly. "*I said, fucking don't*." She'd caught the flash of anger in Yeeb's eyes--the way he was staring knives at Beni.

She'd also noted him surreptitiously yanking out a white tendril that suddenly sprouted from his neck. Now *that* was fucking strange.

Able didn't protest. He recognized the warning in her voice.

Nola noticed the interplay between Able and Death. She realized the prophet wouldn't be hers. The ugly goddess wouldn't permit it.

She smiled demurely at Beni, who, glad to have avoided public humiliation, smiled back in clear relief.

"Yes, Lord Neck, I agree to go with him."

Neck nodded. "Go then."

Nola stepped to Beni's side.

Army head She-kill stepped forward and pointed at Beeli, the first novice initiated. "I would like him," she said.

Neck turned to Beeli, who nodded.

Death turned to Able Kane, smiling her shark's smile. "Come with me. You won't regret it."

Able looked at her narrowly. Was that it, just jealousy?

He stole a last glance at Nola. One hand on her ass, Beni smirked back at him.

Death laughed. "Forget her... them... *Come with me.* You'll be grateful to me later."

Once again, Able recognized the warning in her voice. He got up and escorted Death from the temple, not even minding when she slipped her arm through his.

# VIII.

*Fucking with Death.*

This wasn't going to happen, Able decided, when Death pulled him into the bedroom of their hut. On his own insistence, he'd up till now slept on the living room floor.

No way was he screwing Death. They'd be friends, nothing more; friends for life, even Best Friends Forever, but he wasn't about fucking--

His resolution dissolved once she stripped her catsuit off.

*--that ass? Oh my fucking god!*

He'd imagined what she looked like naked, but the reality flabbergasted him totally. Naked, the sheer gorgeousness of Death's body overrode her face's ugliness entirely. She was sexual unreality itself.

Able found himself suddenly more aroused than he'd been in ages, even with his lemon-headed xombina.

He was even able to kiss Death while they fucked. That was odd, because Death had no lips whatsoever to speak of. His tongue simply slobbered over her sandpapery mouth-rim, slipping between jagged crags of tooth like a raft navigating rapids. Sucking on her tongue felt like eating zombie sausage or jerky.

Her pussy, however, was incredible. Both eating and fucking it.

Its appearance belied its heavenliness. Like her mouth, her cunt was an actual wound--a bleeding knife slash. Her labia were strips of gangrenous meat. Her raw clitoris was covered by a black scab which she peeled off so he could give her head.

Death's cunt stank like a mass grave. The stench was Haeven revisited to Able. He wondered how she concealed it when she walked, seeing as she wasn't wearing any tampon-rats.

As a necros, Able was used to eating filthy pussy. All necros women had cunt odor. In a culture obsessed with the dead and undead, a smelly vagina was considered a cunnilingual necessity, a scent spicing up the main dish.

(Necros men weren't any cleaner where pubic hygiene was concerned. Necros women both considered smegma a delicacy and believed it helped their hair grow longer and stronger. Their husband/boyfriends were expected to have a good stock of foreskin cheese.)

But Death's cunt? Able could visualize the ghosts of the dead she'd killed inside.

But the *feel* when fucking... She was *tight*. He'd never deflowered a virgin before, but he doubted they'd be tighter than Death was.

The tightness took its toll:

"Sorry I didn't wait for you," Able apologized afterward. "Your cunt is simply awesome."

Death giggled. "It's okay... *really*. We'll wait a bit and we'll fuck again. You guys always last longer the second time around anyway."

She was right. The second time he was much more controlled. She came loudly, then he came again.

To revive him, she gave him head.    Able had never had head like that before.    And that was just the start.

He'd never had a woman anything like Death before.

# IX.

Nola initially had reservations about screwing in front of the members of Beni's harem. His two xombinas shambled left and right on their entry, then resumed sitting on their zombie-skin mat, staring expectantly at them.

"It's okay," Beni said. "They like watching humans."

Nola decided necros did what necros did. She climbed onto the bed and waited for him to get undressed.

Copro ceremony over, Nola was uncertain how she felt.

Now she couldn't even remember how the shit had tasted. All she remembered was the afterglow of glorious emotion suffusing her as she licked the fecal cream off her lips.

And Yeeb.

He was here to rescue her she knew. She also somehow knew it was too late.

Beni joined her on the bed. He bent and kissed her. Nola kissed him back. She didn't find it strange that she enjoyed doing so and that she wasn't feeling guilty about betraying Yeeb.

After a while, she didn't think of Yeeb at all.

By that after-a-while, her cunt felt like it was burning. She pulled Beni on top of her.

"Come inside me," she said. "I'm soaking wet."

"Just a minute." Beni pulled on a condom worm and inserted himself into her.

Their bodies moved over each other.

"Shit!" Nola gasped loudly, after an especially deep thrust.

Beni looked at her worriedly.

"Did I hurt you?"

She gasped again. "No. *Harder!* Necro be praised."

Beni concealed his satisfaction. He did as she requested, rolling them both over on their sides.

The significance of his victory wasn't lost on him. Nola looked more than a little like Morphia. Able Kane was definitely fuming now at being denied her.

Nola groaned some more and came violently, a summation of this most transitional week in her life. At this moment, she didn't fucking care about Yeeb or the rest of the fucking universe. What she did know was she'd been primed like a brainshit bomb about to explode.

She exploded now, felt total calm.

#

Beni repositioned himself between her legs and began eating her. Nola floated off somewhere blissful. She gripped Beni's head with both hands, tried to force his tongue deeper inside her.

Then she heard the rustle of the zombie flesh door-strips. She opened her eyes and saw Yeeb there, holding a sword high. His eyes glittered with hatred and rage.

Nola tensed. She removed her hands from Beni's head and stretched them out towards Yeeb.

"No, no, no!" she whispered hoarsely, trapped between pleasure and horror.

Beni once again thought he'd hurt her. He raised his head to look at her, saw she was looking at something behind him, and attempted turning around to see what it was.

Yeeb decapitated him with a single swipe of his sword.

Beni's head rolled off his neck, off the bed, and bounced on the floor. His body collapsed forward between Nola's legs. Blood spurted from his truncated neck into her yawning cunt.

Nola somehow refrained from screaming. She wasn't about yelling in fright, but in anger. What the...?

What restrained her from screaming her anger, however, was seeing how odd Yeeb looked now. From having a crew cut the last time she'd seen him, a week ago, his head was now covered in long thick tendrils; his arms also. Tendrils which wiggled like worms. There was something familiar about the growths too. Nola realized where she'd seen the like before.

Blood potatoes. *Had Yeeb been eating fucking vegan food?* She'd warned him not to try it.

Yeeb placed a hand to his lips. He secured his sword in his belt, then bent and pulled Beni's corpse off Nola. He winced at the sight of her blood-filled vagina. "Get dressed and let's go!" he whispered urgently.

It was then that Nola knew she'd altered for good.

*"Go? Where?"* Her words reflected her thoughts. She was suddenly unable to conceive of anyplace else as home, other than where she currently was--Death Raft 4.

"I've nowhere other than here." She slowly got off the bed. Beni's blood streamed out of her cunt like pee, ran down her legs. She ignored it in necros pride.

Yeeb was speechless. He'd expected any response but *this*. *Nola unwilling to be rescued?*

He reached into a pocket and pulled out a blood potato, took a bite. Nola winced as Yeeb's tendril covering instantly increased.

His tendrils whiplashed right and left around him.

Nola picked up Beni's head and licked the blood from his neck. It stained her lips red like lipstick.

Yeeb flinched in horror. *"What* are you doing? Fucking stop that!" he whispered hoarsely. "Fuck! They've brainwashed you."

Nola took another lick of blood. "No. I am necros now, and you Yeeb, are excrement. No, that dignifies you--you are less that the shit currently in my ass. You're not even fit to lick my anus clean now. Your heresy would defile me. None who refuse to worship zombie are of any value in this re-creation."

Yeeb was stumped. She *was* brainwashed. *Had there been a drug in the black bitch's shit?*

"Look," he whispered gently. "I know I don't know what you've been through in the past week, but we've really got to leave now." He pointed to Beni's body. "Sooner or later, someone will come looking for him."

He felt really odd now. More tendrils had sprouted on his penis again and were badly itching. In addition, his head felt strange, like his mind was contracting and expanding. He pulled out a blood potato and bit into it. Eating more of them seemed the only way to combat the strange feelings they were giving him. Two tendrils instantly sprouted from the left side of his upper lip like a one-sided moustache. He ignored them.

"C'mon, Nola, let's go."

Nola sat back down on the bed, cradling Beni's head to her like a baby. "You go, less-than-shit person. I'm staying here."

Yeeb decided he'd talked enough. He walked over to Nola and pulled her off the bed. "I don't know what they did to you, but we don't have time for--"

She pushed him away violently. Yeeb staggered back. He regained his balance, then stared at Nola like she was mad. "What...?"

"Get lost."

"You're *seriously* not coming?"

"*No*. Go, you son-of-a-bitch. You're lucky I don't sound the alarm on your less-than-shit ass."

Yeeb didn't move. He was shocked. "But..."

"But *what*? I already told you, you're no use now even as toilet paper." She smiled sadly. "It's touching that you came here for me, but you must leave now. I'll wait ten minutes to be sure you've gotten away before I sound the alarm."

"But..."

"Leave, or I'll call the fucking guards on you!"

Yeeb left simmering, his tendrils whipping around him like they were also angry.

Nola watched him go. Then she glared over at Beni's two xombina concubines. "Listen you two pieces of shit, if either of you attempt giving me away, I'll fucking rip you to pieces. Get it?"

"Yessss, Massterrr!!!"

## X.

Able was fucking Death in the ass when he heard Nola's screams. He moved to pull his cock out of her, but Death held him tight, refusing to let him leave her embrace. To reinforce her point, she locked her legs around his waist.

"Forget them and fuck me," she said, smiling. "I told you, you'd be grateful you left with me instead. I think you just got your old job back."

Able totally forgot Nola Fali. Death was too good to give up for some newly promoted under-my-shit person.

He was becoming deeply addicted to Death.

## XI.

Yeeb snuck away from the raft in a black mood. He was mad, disgusted and incensed all rolled into one. *Fuuucccck!* He'd risked his life to save Nola and she'd thrown him out like trash. No, it wasn't *her*. The fucking necros had brainwashed her. The assholes would pay, pay dearly.

The meat-tendrils growing from him lashed the air violently as he climbed down off Death Raft 4 and padded back to his hoverbus.

He was grateful he'd not mentioned the bomb to Nola. She might have tried warning *them*.

His mind ran back over the times they'd shared. Laughing, screwing, kissing... Immediately the image of Nola licking shit from the obese black bitch's ass superimposed itself over his memories.

Yeeb was livid beyond belief. The necros would die, die, die.

Unbelievably furious now, eating blood potato after blood potato, he began furiously priming his bus-bomb.

His body was now altering at an alarming rate, white tendrils sprouting inside his clothes to such an extent he was forced to remove them and work naked.

He no longer bothered himself with plucking them off.

He was bothered by one small question: Why was he repeatedly priming his vehicle-bomb, when he'd set it up perfectly before setting out on this trip?

All he needed to do now was: Aim it at Death Raft 4... remote-control... Boom!

But the potato fever/pain was in his head, and it kept him working and working and working.

Yeeb checked the wiring of his brainshit detonators a hundred times, each time finding it more and more difficult to concentrate on doing so. He kept eating blood potatoes, totally unaware of the changes occurring to his body.

His arms and legs slowly shrunk, as did his neck, while the tendrils covering him grew out longer and became thicker, groups of smaller ones fusing to make larger ones. His neck disappeared completely, leaving his head directly connected to his body. His mouth, ears and nose dissolved into his flesh.

Finally Yeeb's arms and legs were mere vague impressions, leaving his hands and feet appearing directly connected to his body like his head.

His brain dissolved into his body meat, and his eyes blackened into twin sightless beads.

He collapsed back onto the floor, writhing.

Yeeb had become a monster-sized blood potato. His mind gone, he lay in the midst of his bomb-rigged hoverbus and vegetated, his tendrils wriggling madly.

## XII.

The necros never figured out who'd killed Beni. Nola gave them an accurate description of Yeeb, and many necros remembered seeing him at the shit-licking initiation, but he was nowhere to be found on the hovervillage.

Then Death explained that Yeeb had been a divine assassin, sent by Necro himself to assassinate Beni, who was secretly a heretic. His job done, he'd returned to Haeven.

The priests immediately seized on her explanation and began vociferously lobbying for Able Kane to be restored to his former office. Necro had clearly killed Beni because he wished his chosen messenger to resume his duties.

They did this not because they disliked Able any less, but because if he was back processing food, he'd clearly not have any time to meddle in religious affairs.

(Hopefully, his being out of the public's eye would keep him out of their religious consciousness also.)

On Death's prompting, Able grudgingly accepted his old job back.

Nola chose another necros partner after Death made it VERY clear to her she'd wither her to ash if she made a nuisance of herself over Able.

## XIII.

Death Raft 4 left Salt Lake the next afternoon, the necros never even seeing Yeeb's explosion-primed hoverbus.

All around them the world kept changing.

And as it changed, Able Kane was plagued by God's words about his people's 'hour of direst need.'

It was coming soon, that he was VERY certain of.

# Chapter 7

Soil grew tired of feeding on the vegfarms. There were too many little humanosaurs trampling everywhere and getting under her feet.

She turned her attention to the worlderness--to the necros' Death Rafts. She smelled food out there, lots of delicious human food.

The sun was hot and blazing when she began stomping her way toward Death Raft 4.

#

On the Utah Plains, Yeeb-potato still lay vegetating in the middle of the bomb-rigged hoverbus.

Soil, the womanosaur, stamped on the hoverbus and flattened it cardboard thin (mashing Yeeb-potato into Yeeb-potato paste) on her way to feed on the necros.

# Chapter 8

## *Return of/to the Sun.*

Amidst a crowd of necros, Able Kane stood hand in hand with Death, watching the approaching humanosaur.

Though still fifty miles away, Soil dominated the landscape like a mountain.

"*In their hour of direst need, my sun will come and deliver them,*" Death whispered to him. "I think your hour of direst need is walking towards us at a mile a minute. There's no way in Hell's fires we're stopping this thing without divine intervention." She looked pointedly at Able. "I just hope meatball wasn't head-fuckin' with your ass."

Able looked at her sharply. "Don't blaspheme," he said softly. "We're in enough trouble as it is."

"I don't worship your god," Death replied. "We've got major employer/employee issues."

"*What* issues?"

"The cheapskate refused to pay me enough to fear him unconditionally."

Able said nothing. Overhead the sun grew hotter and hotter.

\#

Soil came closer and closer. The necros crowding Able and Death parted in an aisle to let Neck through to stand beside them.

"It's time," the god priest said. "Now everything comes to pass."

There were four other death rafts flanking Death Raft 4. The elite of the necros army stood in these, armed to the teeth with weaponry which even in their minds was pathetically inadequate.

*How could an ant destroy a hammer?*

Soil came nearer and yet nearer still. She yawned, spreading jaws wide enough to engulf each Death Raft whole. She was that immense now.

The necros grew uneasy, threatening to break and flee.

"Now we chant," Neck said.

She stood out ahead of Able and Death on the raft and began to intone: "Necro, Necro, Necro!"

Her chant was copied by Able and the other necros on Death Raft 4. It spread like wildfire to the necros on the other rafts.

Their voices became a mighty thunder under the searing sun.

#

When Soil was a mile from the raft, it happened.

Everything turned black for an instant, like during an eclipse.

When there was light again, all the necros turned to look up at the sun.

All stared in shock.

The sun had become a bright blue eye.

Instinctively, the chants of 'Necro' grew louder and louder.

The sun-eye blinked. Its pupil widened into a wide mouth full of teeth. From the mouth's edges two flaps of flesh extended into transparent hands that reached down from the sky and picked up Soil.

Soil fought against the hands. She squealed and bit and scratched, but was powerless to halt the inexorable forces lifting her up. The hands dwarfed her as completely as she in turn dwarfed the necros.

The sun's hands raised Soil up to its toothy mouth far above the world.

Suddenly appreciating the danger she was in, Soil stopped fighting and began screaming in fear.

Her struggles forced her cuntbag zip open, spilling uneaten corpses earthward.

(Momentarily, the fog of dinosaur flesh-lust cleared from Soil's mind and she could think clearly. She was able to appreciate what was about to happen to her--how she was about to die.

Her realization of her impending end, however, made no difference to the outcome, other than to fill her with heart-wrenching horror and terror.)

The eye's hands placed her head-first between its lips and with a violent wrench, bit off her head.

Blood pumped from her severed neck, from her huge blood vessels. It rained down on the necros.

The eye chewed Soil's head to break its bones, then swallowed it.

Slowly, the mouth in the sun-eye ate the rest of the womanosaurus, now biting her apart as delicately as the DEZA queen eating a potato.

As it consumed their enemy, the necros screamed and yelled and entered convulsions of joy. They slashed themselves with their knives to show the depth and truth of their worship.

Soil was almost all gone now. Only her legs projected from the eye's pupil, kicking involuntarily in remembered reflexes. Then they too disappeared into the mouth in the eye.

The loud sound of eye-teeth crunching her bones fell on the world.

The sun-eye burped. It blinked again and was back to normal, burning the sky again.

"Necro be praised!" Neck screamed at the sky.

"NECRO BE PRAISED!" The thousand necros on the raft screamed.

"Necro be praised!" Able Kane whispered.

"Meatball didn't let you guys down after all," Death whispered to Able. She surreptitiously placed his left hand on her ass. "I feel horny, let's go screw."

Able let her lead him away.

*We're all right now*, he thought as they left the crowd, *but for how long?*

#

Later, with Death's ankles up on his shoulders and his cock deep inside her cunt,

Able forgot the huge load of guilt now weighing on him.

But afterwards, while she slept beside him, the guilt returned, magnified.

He *knew* the disaster falling on the re-creation wasn't his fault, but *it was*.

He wondered if everything would have turned out differently, if he'd not fled to Texas, but stayed and meekly accepted the sentence of execution Priest had passed on him.

He grimaced at the thought. Now that *would* have been stupid, wouldn't it?

Epilogue:
One year later in Texas

Able Kane and Death stood staring at the lemon tree.

"You really can't blame them all for wanting to leave," Death said.

Able nodded.

They were standing on the roof of a ruined house near the lemon tree, watching zombies swarm toward it from every direction. The undead all reached the base of the tree and started climbing, ascending it without the aid of a ladder, streaming up its bark like overgrown ants.

"They never come down though," Able said. He patted her belly, feeling the new life there.

Death was pregnant with Able's child. Her belly bulged like a misplaced set of buttocks.

"I think they find the cuntdoors and go into each and every one. Or they're sucked down into them by forces beyond their empty-headed comprehension."

"Shit!" Able yelped. "Look who's here!"

They ducked out of sight as a pack of were-zombie hoverbikers rode into view, zooming over the broken-up ancient road.

The were-zombie bikers wore gore-smeared human-leather clothes. A few had viscera spilling out of their biker jackets.

Their wolf-eyes gleamed blood-red. Their wolf-mouths slobbered saliva over their long yellow teeth.

They spoke to each other in canine yelps and growls, and occasionally raised their snouts and howled lustily at the sky.

The were-zombies carried weapons that were neither vegan nor necros, odd guns that ran on alien principles.

With the DEZA gone, the were-zombies and their pillion-riding bitch-girls ruled all the worlderness except for the necros lands.

(Both cultures were permanently at each other's throats, with neither gaining an upper hand.

The were-zombies were stronger and faster, but the necros were simply too expert at killing zombies. The necros welcomed the conflicts--were-zombie flesh could be eaten without the usual week-long menstrual-blood purification, and also had medicinal properties.)

The were-zombies were lean, mean, and obscene.

They were omnivores, eating human, zombie or humanosaurus meat indiscriminately (to the disgust of the necros, who now that zombies thronged the earth in their millions, gloried in Necro's prescribed diet for mankind).

Were-zombies even considered brain skin a delicacy, making it the meal of honor at their marriage rut festivals.

They ate vegetables also.

Now, while Able and Death peeked out at them, the zombie werewolf bikers shot and hacked a section of the zombie mob at the base of the lemon tree into chunks. They loaded the mass of zombie flesh into a hovercart they'd brought along especially for this purpose.

Several of them pulled their bitches off their bikes and started fucking them on the ground. Those others not involved in packing meat cheered them on.

Able was unable to contain his disgust at the bikers.

"They're beasts, total animals."

Death smirked, her shark-mouth setting in a grin. "Whatever happened to them being the pure crown of Necro's creation?"

"That was when they'd just emerged from the lemon tree," Able countered defensively. "Now they've also become corrupted by Hereticos."

Death giggled. She rubbed her pregnancy against Able's hand. "Hereticos seems to corrupt everything that enters the worlderness. Are you sure you humans aren't the real bad influence?"

Able fumed. He, now a recognized pillar of the necros faith, still found it hard accepting the fact that his goddess girlfriend was a heretic.

His mind perpetually boggled at the oxymoron concept--how could a deity be a religious skeptic? They'd both been to Haeven after all. And she, apparently, not for the first time.

Able stared wistfully up the tree connecting Haeven and earth. "Maybe we'll go there again."

"Huh?"

"Haeven. We could go visit again after the kid's born."

Death regarded him narrowly. "You're not looking to fuck God again are you--lusting after meatball's ass?" She pulled away from him, her ugly face setting into an uglier frown.

Able winced. *Women.* He smiled. "C'mon, baby, don't be like that." He pulled her close, keeping up a gentle pressure till she gave in and snuggled nicely against him again. "That's better."

They resumed watching the fucking were-zombies, the bitch-girls yelping their doggy orgasms.

"They help us take care of the human-dinosaurs," the God-Priest Neck had pointed out once to Able.

Which was true: With EVERYTHING ultra fucked-up now, the were-zombie arrival on the worlderness stage had brought a new sort of balance.

For one thing, their alien weapons could *kill* the humanosauruses.

Which made a *hell* of a lot of difference.

#

"Dunno 'bout you," Death giggled suddenly," but watching those things fuck has got me in the mood also. Let's..."

She raised her skirt, slid her panties aside, and they did it standing, with her looking over the wall to keep watch on the were-zombies.

Later, when the zombie werewolves had biked off again, Death and Able left Texas.

They rode east, in the opposite direction to the were-zombie pack, through a motley assortment of old towns, heading for Texarkana, the new necros headquarters.

Since the vegan implosion and zombie werewolf advent, necros civilization had steadily shifted from a nomadic to an urbanized culture. Forts were easier to defend against humanosaur and were-zombie attacks than death rafts.

Death tapped Able's shoulder just as they were leaving Zurich.

"Pull over," she hissed in his ear, "gotta pee already."

He did so, stopping the hoverbike beside the roofless hulk of a house with moss-covered walls. Death got off quickly and squatted a distance away.

Where childbirth was concerned, there was little difference between the biological mechanics of goddesses and mortal women. The abnormal weight of the baby on Death's bladder had been augmented by her pushing her belly against Able's back as she rode pillion to him.

The result: A stream of pee she was glad to be rid off.

She peed facing Able, so he could see it, smiling like a little girl doing something really naughty.

Able laughed back. Despite her dramatic mood shifts (and their associated drama), pregnant Death was a bundle of fun. He waved their were-zombie dino-gun at her. "Mind you don't pee our kid out."

Death giggled and concentrated to squeeze every last drop out so they wouldn't need to stop again before they hit Texarkana.

She was heaving a final sigh of relief when the humanosaurus rushed around the side of the building.

It happened so fast, Able Kane never knew what hit him.

He never stopped smiling at her.

"Watch out!" Death screamed helplessly, as the womanosaur's huge jaws split and clamped shut over Able's head and chest, biting him completely in two. His severed hands fell to the ground, the gun he'd been holding clanging dully as it hit the rocky desert floor.

The womanosaur reared up again, chewing what she had in her mouth.

The bottom half of Able's body, temporarily still attached to its top half by a single strand of intestine, fell off the bike.

Death froze, paralyzed with shock now. *Not-a-fucking-gain.*

The womanosaur finished swallowing Able's head and arms, then picked up the rest of him. Squatting, she stuffed Able's ass and legs into her cuntbag, gathered up his hands and did the same with them, then zipped herself up neatly. She was saving these for when she was hungry later.

She noticed the squatting pregnant woman then, and peered at her inquisitively.

Death read the blocked ID on her head. 69f.

The womanosaur sniffed the air coming from Death, then instantly lost interest in her.

Death wasn't human. She smelled totally wrong for food.

The womanosaur turned and bounded off into the distance.

Death finally unfroze. She got to her feet and staggered over to the blood spattered bike. She picked up the dino-gun and aimed it after the departing 69f, but the womanosaur was already too distant to hit.

#

Death was totally disgusted by the turn of events.

She shed no tears over Able's passing.

She pulled her panties off and made herself comfortable on the bike. Then, none-too-carefully, she spread her gangrenous labia and forced her hand up into her cunt.

Bending over like a contortionist, she worked the hand all the way up the passage, till it passed her cervix and she could feel her baby's head.

Smiling grimly, Death slipped her fingers around the head. Its soft bones depressed as she took firm hold of it.

Then, with a howl like those the were-zombies made fucking in full-moon rut, Death yanked her child out of her body. It exited in a stream of stinky pink pus.

She whimpered from the pain of its abortion--it had quite a big head.

She dropped the fetus on the ground by the bike and felt up inside herself again, tracing its placenta to its roots in her front womb wall. She dug her fingers deep into its spongy material, and yanked it out also.

She dropped it beside the child. Then she sat, panting heavily and regarded the fetus.

Even only three-quarters developed, the child had Able's face. It was a boy. She could see the tiny matchstick penis between its legs.

Its mouth, though, would have been hers, a knife-wound slash filled with teeth more suited to a ravening sea dweller.

She grunted while the pain in her belly subsided.

The child twitched its semblance of pre-birth life. Death shrugged at it. "Sorry kid, hating to do this to ya, but with your daddy dead, you're just excess luggage."

She got down off the bike and killed the fetus, placing her heel on its head and stamping downwards, so its brains sprayed out sideways from under her sole.

She wiped her foot dry on the sand. She wiped her pussy clean with her panties and threw them away.

Before getting on the hoverbike and speeding across the worlderness to Texarkana to inform the necros of Able Kane's death, Death buried her abortion beneath a makeshift upside-down cross.

She knew either a were-zombie or humanosaur would dig it up later and eat it, but that couldn't be helped.

At least the kid had gotten a burial, which was more than its father had.

Death would have eaten the fetus herself, but she felt that would have been disrespectful to Able Kane.

She had loved him after all.


The End.

## About The Author:

Wol-vriey is Nigerian, and quite tall.

He currently resides in a state of uneasy stalemate with his threatening-to-thin-beyond-redemption hair, and believes there actually are things that go bump in the night.

Wol-vriey recycles the ridiculous into reasonable reality for the reader. His WEIRRRD philosophy? WEIRRRD = Warp/Write Everything into Realistic Ridiculous Readable Distorted Dream Dimension Descriptions.

Wol-vriey blogs at
http://oddityfarm.wordpress.com

# OTHER GREAT TITLES FROM

# THE
# BIG
# BOOK
# OF
# BIZARRO

JAM PACKED
OVER
**50**
WEIRD TALES

## EDITED BY
## RICH BOTTLES JR. AND GARY LEE VINCENT

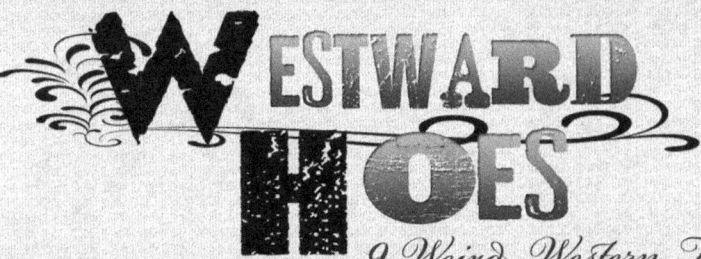

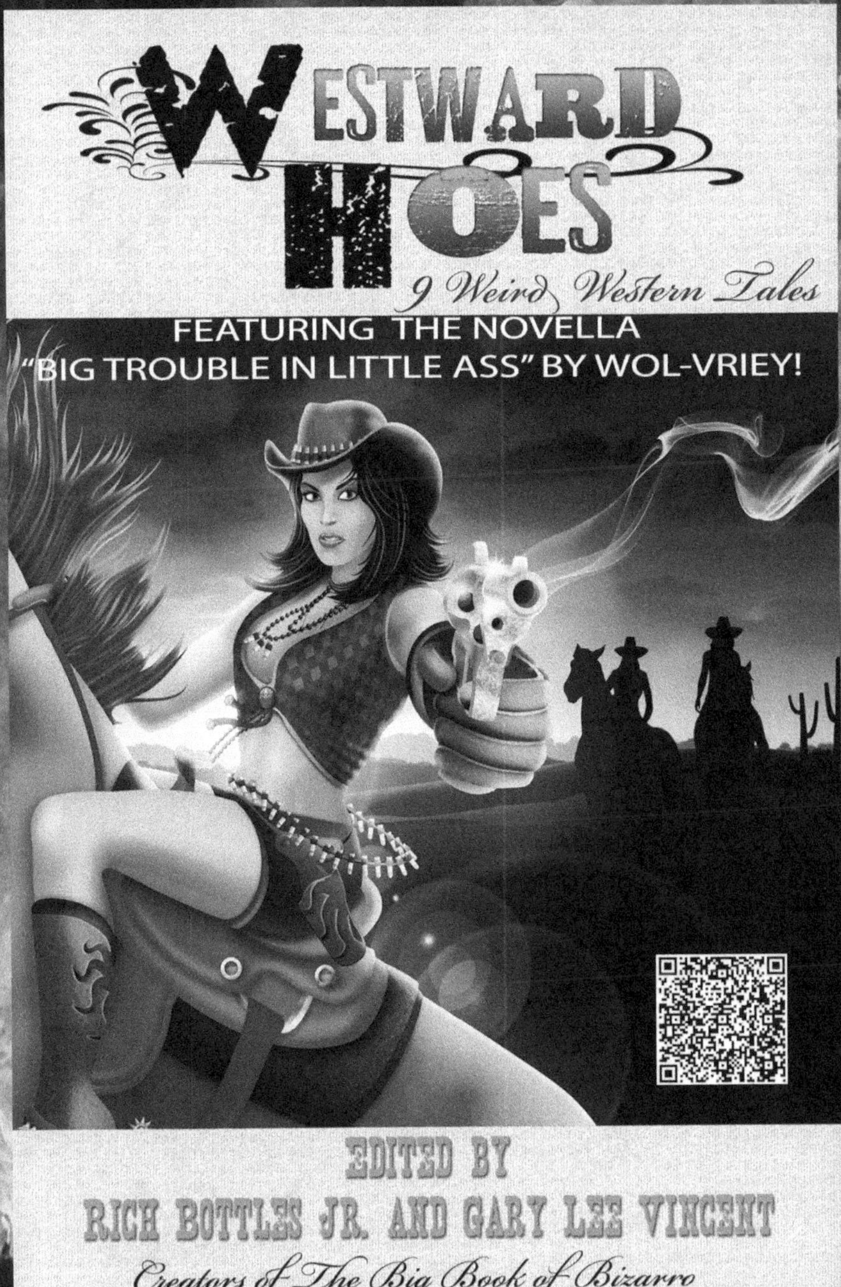
WESTWARD
HOES
9 Weird Western Tales
FEATURING THE NOVELLA
“BIG TROUBLE IN LITTLE ASS” BY WOL-VRIEY!
EDITED BY
RICH BOTTLES JR. AND GARY LEE VINCENT
Creators of The Big Book of Bizarro

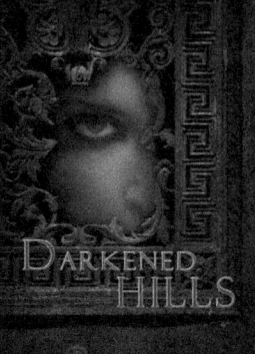

# RICH BOTTLES JR.

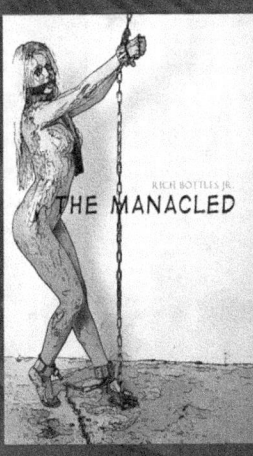

## WEST VIRGINIA
## HUMORROROTICA

# VULGARITY FOR THE MASSES

## J.S. LAWHEAD

www.ingramcontent.com/pod-product-compliance
Lightning Source LLC
Chambersburg PA
CBHW070806180626
46818CB00001B/123